NOT EVERYTHING IS LIKE IT SEEMS

Katarzyna Nowocin-Kowalczyk

NOT EVERYTHING IS LIKE IT SEEMS

Life-written Fairy Tales for Adults

Translated from the Polish by

Elizabeth Kanski

ISBN: 979-8-9859777-4-5

Title: Not Everything Is Like It Seems
Original title: Nie wszystko jest takie, jak nam się wydaje
Author: Katarzyna Nowocin-Kowalczyk

Translated from the Polish by Elizabeth Kanski
Edited by Elizabeth Kanski
Illustrations Marek Szczęsny
Cover design by Kay Umland

Second edition
First printing 2022

Published by Katarzyna Nowocin-Kowalczyk

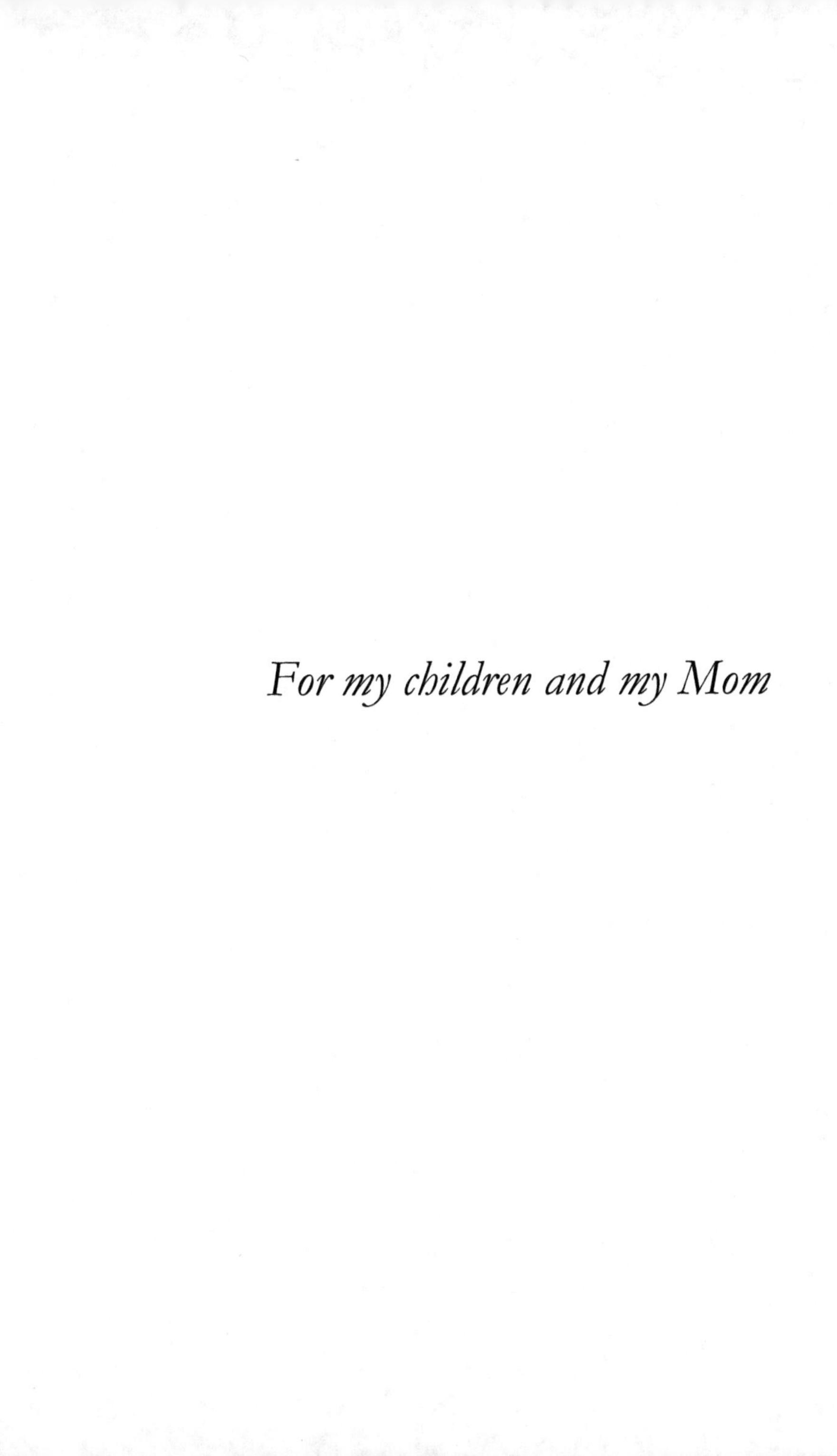

For my children and my Mom

From the author

When you listen to Silence, you hear that this Silence speaks. Suddenly the wind, the water, the bird, the tree, the flower, and even the mirror or bench in the park tell you their story.

When you listen to Silence, you hear yourself. The whispering of your soul. You discover a New World. New lands. New ports. You discover the unknown. That, which is hidden from the world of matter. What the eyes do not see. You experience a fascinating journey into yourself. An amazing, cosmic journey into the depths of the Universe. Because your soul is the Universe.

And then you understand that all is One. Everything is intertwined. One is a reflection of the other. One symbolizes the other, although seemingly very distant. The eyes of the soul see more. And then you understand that what you see with earthly eyes is just an illusion of cinema. You understand that Nothing is as it seems to be.

Katarzyna (Catherine) Nowocin-Kowalczyk

Matrix

I sleep, or I no longer sleep
Is a Dream Wakefulness
Is Wakefulness a Dream
What is True, what a Dream
Is a Dream an Illusion
When I wake up
I just fall asleep
I sleep or no longer sleep
Is Wakefulness a Dream
Or someone's Game
And I a Character
Believing that it is Me
But after all, not Me
Freedom is in Dream
I am flying high
And I see more
And do what I want
Without Pain and Tears
Two worlds but One
World of Truth and Dream
But is a Dream a Dream
What is Truth, what is Dream
And is Me Me
Katarzyna Nowocin-Kowalczyk

Contents

NOT EVERYTHING IS LIKE IT SEEMS

Not Everything Is Like It Seems

An exclusive hotel in Beverly Hills. A friend invited me to a private concert of a well-known artist. We met earlier to have dinner and talk. And we never lack common, interesting topics. We are sitting sit at a table and to the sounds of gentle live music from the piano standing nearby, we are enjoying really good coffee. At some point, the friend receives an important phone call from his business partner who has just flown in from London and is staying at the same hotel. My friend apologizes and goes out to the lobby for a moment to say hello to him. He had warned me before that such a situation could happen, so I accept it with understanding.

At the next table, also with a cup of coffee, there is an attractive, well-groomed woman with Asian features. She may be about forty-something years old. She looks like she's waiting for someone or something. You can see that she is a bit tense. Our eyes meet. We exchange smiles.

"You have a very beautiful accent," she says in English with a Californian accent. Her voice sounds pleasant, while the way of speaking and gestures indicate a person with education and manners. "I love it. Can I ask where you are from?"

"I am Polish."

"Really? I heard that Poland is a beautiful country. Two years ago, my boyfriend and I were in Europe. We visited several countries, but we did not reach Poland, although we had plans. We ran out of time. We were in Prague. It's so beautiful there."

Americans often think that once they have reached Prague it means that they know Central and Eastern Europe. They talk about the Prague Castle, Charles Bridge, the Old Town, Visegrad Hill, delicious dumplings and delicious beer. The Czechs are indeed great at selling themselves... And I, too often, can't help but to say that Prague was not destroyed during the Second World War, as Warsaw and—depending on the situation and the interlocutor—I start my shorter or longer stories about beautiful Poland and its difficult, albeit very interesting history.

For a moment we talk about Europe and the places she has visited. Of course, I invite her to Poland and, as it is usually in similar situations, for a moment I become an ambassador of my country. My interlocutor actually turns out to be an educated woman. She tells me that although she graduated from a prestigious university with a degree in history of art, which is still her passion, she does something completely different. Together with her boyfriend they run an elegant restaurant and are just planning to open another one. I am a cultural expert by education, and my first diploma was in hotel and restaurant management, so a thread of understanding is established between us very quickly. I invite the woman to my table. We engage in conversation, and the muse Klio spreads her protective wings over us. We are so absorbed in ourselves and our subjects that we do not notice when my Friend appears at the table. We start laughing when he suddenly pops up next to us, like from under the ground.

I introduce them. The woman gets up and tactfully wants to return to her table. We invite her to stay, though. We still have some time before the concert starts. My friend orders a bottle of good Californian Cabernet. Despite the interesting conversation, the fact doesn't escape our attention that the new acquaintance, although she tries very hard to control it, still seems excited about something, and at the same time a bit distracted and tense. Finally, I say:

"Sorry to ask, but did anything happen? You look like you're waiting for something you're afraid of."

A surprised look and a moment of silence. You can see a thought on her face—to say, to throw it out of yourself, or not? After all, we are strangers to her. But it has been known for a long time that it is easiest to talk in front of strangers. Strangers do not judge, and the heart gets lighter. All the more so because we may never meet again. The woman reaches for the bulbous glass and drinks a sip of red liquor. As if she wanted to gain time.

"This wine is really good. You can feel our Californian sun and earth in it," then looking straight into my eyes she says seriously, albeit with a gentle smile. "You read people well. I knew from the beginning that you were a good observer."

Now I'm smiling.

"Let's say I know a little bit about human nature."

"Yes. I'm really waiting for something. For a meeting. And I'm a little scared of it."

"Would you like to tell us about it?"

"If you want to listen, I guess so. I guess I have to throw it out. I've been thinking about it since yesterday, but it's really my whole life. I'm still confused..."

"Tell us. We will be happy to listen," says my Friend gently, whose one of the many traits is empathy.

The woman reaches for the glass again. This time, she looks as if collecting thoughts. We give her time. If something bothers you all life, it means that it hurts, that it is something difficult and it is not easy to talk about it.

"I was born in China. I lived there in an orphanage. I was adopted by my current parents when I was seven years old. I was put on a plane alone and told to fly to an unknown country and strangers...I remember being very afraid. I cried. I didn't want to come here. Although in the orphanage it was nightmarish. Rigor, fear and loneliness. And often hunger...Penalties for even the slightest offense... I saw my adoptive parents for the first time at LAX airport... For the first time, someone hugged me so tightly...and kissed...Over time, this foreign country became my country, and strangers became the best parents I could have dreamed of..."

Tears appear in the woman's eyes. In mine, too. This time we both reach for the wine...

"How did it happen that you ended up in an orphanage? What about your biological parents? "I ask.

"I have been asking myself this question all my life. Not a day did go by that I didn't think about it. Bad thoughts. I asked—what was wrong with me that they didn't want me? Why didn't they love me? I was given away when I was one year old. I don't remember my biological parents."

"But something has happened recently, hasn't it?"

"You really have a good intuition—a smile. Yes. It has changed...Some time ago, my boyfriend persuaded me to do DNA tests. Our data were automatically included in the database. Two weeks ago, I got a call. It was my nephew, who I didn't know existed. My older sister's son. I didn't know about her either…I didn't know anything about myself...And it was terrible...Not knowing what your roots are...What a story... Who are you alike...After whom you have eyes, smile, and after whom one or another trait...My adoptive parents are dear and I know that they love me very much... But they're white, and I'm Asian... I don't look like them..." The woman thinks for a moment. Her unseeing eyes indicate that for this brief moment she is somewhere far away. However, she quickly returns to the here and now. "My cousin was calling from London. It turned out that they were looking for me... And they found me through these DNA tests."

"What about the orphanage? They couldn't ask for information there?"

"This orphanage is gone. It turned out that it burned down a few years after I left. And with it all the documentation. It was a great tragedy. Many children also died then. I didn't know that until yesterday."   "And what happened yesterday?"

"Yesterday I met my sister, her husband and my nephew who called me and my cousin...Especially for me they flew to Los Angeles from London...To see me...Meet me..."

"And how did you feel?"

"I don't know...Strange...But I'm happy...It's still hard for me to recover...It all happened so suddenly, unexpectedly and in such a short time...Today I am to meet my brother...

"Have you found answers to your questions?" my Friend asks.

"Yes...I guess so... I don't know...But a lot became clear..."

"Do you already know why you ended up in an orphanage?"

"It turned out that when I was less than a year old my father left my mother with four small children for another woman. He disappeared...We lived in a small town. A lonely woman abandoned by her husband was a shame and a kind of stigma. Mom had trouble finding a job and securing our upkeep. All the more so because the children were small. She had to ask for help from her father, my grandfather. He was wealthy. And it was he who ruled. Mom obeyed him in everything. That's how she was raised. Such was the reality.

Anyway, until today this is the Chinese tradition and culture. I have two older brothers and a sister. I was the youngest. It was my grandfather who gave me away to an orphanage. Reportedly Mom cried but was afraid to object. He forbade her to contact me. He said it was for her and my good. He reportedly wanted to help her. Older children could work but I had to be taken care of."

"Did you have the chance to contact your biological mother?"

"My Mom is dead. She died many years ago. When my siblings left for the UK. Apparently, for the rest of her life she worried about me...Maybe it's hard for you to believe, but I felt it...I've dreamed about her many times...She sang me a song...always the same...I don't remember her face, but I remember the smile...and the smell...I missed her so much...Grandpa also died..."

"What about your father? Was he found?"

"Yes. A year ago. Also, in London. He was the one who found my siblings. Unfortunately, he died of a heart attack before meeting them. But they went to his funeral. Then it turned out that he was a very prosperous businessman and created a large international company. Now it is managed by one of my brothers. The one I'm about to meet today. The other brother lives in Amsterdam and is engaged in scientific work. I haven't met him yet, but we were on the phone..."

Sipping the drink of Gods, the woman becomes thoughtful again.

"What an unpredictable life it is...We were born somewhere in the Chinese countryside, theoretically with no prospects for the future and despite difficult beginnings we all graduated from good universities and became successful...They also went through a lot...I always thought that my mother didn't want me, she didn't love me...and the truth was completely different..."

Tears flow down her cheeks...

"What is your brother's name?" This unexpected question from my Friend surprises both of us. The stunned woman gives his first and last names.

"Why do you ask? Do you know him?"

"Yes. Your brother is my business partner. I was just greeting him in the lobby. I also knew your father. I did business with him, but your father, first of all, was my friend. And I was also at his funeral."

"Did you know my father?!" The woman's great surprise is mixed with curiosity.

"Yes."

...

"And I know this story..., but from a different side..."

"What was he like?" the woman asks after she gets her bearing.

"An idealist... He was a big idealist...And a good, honest man."

"A good man? Does a good man leave his wife and children for another woman and not give a sign of life?"

"Your father said, 'The poor are afraid of relatives, and the rich are afraid of thieves.'"

"And?"

"He also said: 'In fragments, there is little truth or no truth at all.'"

"I already know the truth. And I know what I've been through."

"You've been through a lot. But you yourself said that life is unpredictable. It writes its own scripts. Often, to be good, it is difficult at first. Life hardens and teaches. It gives lessons. The winner is the one who does that homework."

"But why do small children suffer?"

"Who knows who you would be now and where you would be if it weren't for what happened in your early childhood..."

"But this doesn't justify my father. He left us and my mother...Because what? Because he fell in love? Is this what a responsible man does? Good - as you called him."

"Yes, he left you. But he didn't do it of his own free will. And certainly not for another woman. Your father was alone. There was only one woman in his life. Your mother."

"How's that? What are you talking about? So why did he leave?"

"The heart of man is like iron, but the law is like a furnace that melts it','" these are the words of your father. He often said this."

"But what does this have to do with me and my family?"

"It has more than you suppose. Your father and I often played golf. We both liked it very much. I still like it. "With these words, my Friend, who was born and raised in Great Britain, smiles gently. I know very well that he is a golf fan. Such is his English whim. Sometimes we play together, but I'll probably never match him in skills and precision of throws. "Golf is a game that brings you closer. It builds a kind of trust. Once, after about an 18-hole round, when he kicked my ass quite well—unfortunately it was not my good day on the course—your father, wanting to improve my mood, invited me to his place for a drink. And as we sat at his place on the terrace, he opened up and told me his story. That was the only time we talked about it. I could see that this was a very difficult subject for him, which he tried to deal with until his death."

"Will you tell me this story?"

"Yes. You have the right to know the truth...I think he would like that." After a moment of silence, my Friend begins the story, which the intrigued woman is waiting for. I admit that me, as well. "Your father and your mother loved each other very much. Unfortunately, your father came from a not very wealthy family. In addition, he was suspected of anti-government activity, which was not without truth. Your grandfather did not like all of this. He found another candidate for your mom. Your parents got married in secret. Grandpa was furious. He cut himself off from them, even though your mom was his only child. Your eldest brother was born, then your sister, your other brother, and finally you. Your grandfather did not visit his daughter even once. He didn't want to meet all of you. He also didn't let your mom in when she went to him with her first child. It was not easy for your parents, but they managed. Your father was an educated man, although he did not have a diploma. He was expelled from his studies in his final year of history, just before defending his master's thesis. Or rather, not allowed to defend it. As I mentioned earlier, he was suspected of anti-government activity. He even spent several months in a Chinese prison. Since then, he was under strict surveillance. Therefore, he had trouble finding a permanent good job. People were afraid to hire someone like that because they didn't want to get into trouble..." My Friend interrupts his story for a moment and drinks some wine.

"Okay, but why did he disappear so suddenly from our lives?" The woman asks.

"'The poor are afraid of relatives, and the rich are afraid of thieves.' ...He was reported by one of his relatives. No, it wasn't your grandfather. Your grandfather actually protected all of you. For people born in the free world, it is difficult to imagine the fear that people living under the regime of communism experience every day and every night...'The law is like a fence, the tiger will jump over, the rat will slip through, and the cattle is standing.' ...These are also your father's words…He was threatened with arrest and imprisonment, and even death. Also, your mother and all of you as his family...He had to protect you...It was your grandfather who helped him escape the country. Not only did he organize this escape, but he also paid for everything. Of course, everything took place in secret and very quickly. The version about escaping with a woman was the official version. Your mom knew everything too. Unfortunately, you were the victim who was supposed to shut people's mouths. They have never told all of you anything to protect you."

My Friend interrupts his story again, and tears flow down the woman's cheeks again. I take her hand.

"That's why he never wrote us a letter...to protect us...And he could never go back to China..."

"Yes...I once had a business trip to Shanghai. He asked me to give your mom a letter. I went to your village. Unfortunately, neither your mother nor your grandfather were alive. And your siblings left. When I came back, I found out about your dad's passing...It was a shock...Then I forgot about this letter. Until yesterday."

My Friend reaches into the inner pocket of his jacket, pulls out a white envelope and hands it to the woman. "I was supposed to give it to your brother tomorrow, but I think it's you who should get it."

The woman's hands tremble when she opens the envelope and takes out a piece of paper written in Chinese characters.

"Can you read it?" I ask.

"Yes. I know Mandarin. My adoptive parents made sure I never forgot it."

My Friend looks at his watch.

"It's time for us...You should also know that your father spent many years searching for you... to find all you...He hired the best detective agency in London for this purpose. He was so happy when he finally managed to find the trail of your siblings. He was very worried about you...He often wondered what you looked like, what you were like...You were so tiny when he had to leave you..."

"Again, it turned out that not everything is like it seems," the woman says. "Thank you for showing me the truth…"

"Your father once said to me, 'On the day of your birth, everyone was happy, only you wept. Live in such a way that in your last hour everyone else is crying, and you alone will laugh heartily and have no tears in your eye.' Don't cry any more…You were a loved and wanted child. The rest are brutal circumstances created by people. Unfortunately, an evil deed of one man, maybe his Ego, maybe fear, or maybe something else—in this case, your relative—have an influence on many other lives… but these are all lessons… and you made your homework… the most important thing is that you are together again…And as you just said—Do not create truth from fragments, because not everything is like it seems…"

We are leaving. We head to the Hall where the concert is to take place. In the distance we see the woman bent over a sheet of white paper.

Angels

Madrid, early pre-noon. The end of the eighties. My husband and I are going to a social agency to collect our benefits. We are talking about our first child, who settled in my tummy for good, about which we found out a month ago, that is, right after arriving in Spain. My husband jumped for joy, but for me, realizing this fact was, for the first split second, quite a shock. Although it shouldn't. Because as they say –if there is an action there are consequences...It may be worth explaining to those who do not remember or do not know that in those—how distant, although still fresh, as if it were yesterday—times, you could count on three methods of contraception...the intermittent method, the thermometer method and the supplication method, that is, the prayer that it does not happen... However, it has been known for a long time that youth has its rights, blood is not water, and a prayer has not always worked... As probably with more than 90% of other couples...Well, well, you want to make God laugh, tell him about your plans...He knows better what is good for us, although at a given moment, it often seems differently to us.

And why was I shocked for a tiny moment? After all, we talked about the baby, and we wanted to have one. But this moment...Here we are at the beginning of our emigration, a great change in life, an unknown one might say, and here the information about the pregnancy falls on us. What will it be like? To return to Poland or to stay? What a time you chose my son…least appropriate...Well, but what time is appropriate? And when, years later, we look from a distance and in retrospect, it turns out that this time was the most appropriate...even perfect...So, as I used to do in such moments, I immediately turned on the logic and said, ok, we still have a few months...we will have time to prepare and sort everything out somehow...after all I will not give birth on the street...it will be fine...And indeed it was....

"Do you feel well, honey? How is our Helenka doing?" my husband asks. Not knowing why, he insisted on a daughter and "routinely" called her Helenka. Maybe because he had two older brothers himself. So far, I also have no idea if he would actually call her Helenka if in fact a daughter was born.

"Helenka is doing well, only it is not Helenka but a boy." I answer with a smile. He doesn't understand, but we women just know certain things without checking. Some call it intuition.

"There will be Helenka and she will be as beautiful as her mother." Oh, how charming he could be...

End of February. Wonderful, mild Spanish climate. It is relatively warm, although only a month ago we flew here bundled up to the ears, protecting ourselves from Polish frosts. We are already close to the agency. We see the building and the main entrance. One more block and we will reach our destination.

On the street corner, on the sidewalk, a beggar sits by the wall, bundled in some rags. A granny. We've seen her before. Previously when we were here for the first time. Then, concerned about the new situation in which we found ourselves—a new country, emigration, arranging residence documents, housing, etc., plus news about the child—we did not pay much attention to her, although subconsciously we noted her presence. This time it's different. And we don't have to say anything. We understand each other without words. Together we approach the woman. My husband pulls out all the change that we still have left from the last payment. There's not much of it. In total, only a few pesetas. Everything he found in his pockets he throws into a bowl standing on the ground. Well, but in a moment, we will get money. In the meantime, I am observing the woman's tired, furrowed face.

"Tienes hambre? Comiste algo hoy? (Are you hungry? Did you eat something today?)" I ask in Spanish. "No, todavía no he comido nada. (No, I haven't eaten anything yet)."
I reach into my bag and pull out the sandwiches I've prepared for us for the road. We lived in a beautiful university town of Alcala de Henares, about 40 kilometers from Madrid, where we rented an apartment. On that day, taking advantage of the opportunity to stay in the capital, we planned to visit friends, also like us, emigrants from Poland.

I'm handing the sandwiches to the woman.

"Gracias angel (Thank you angel)."

"De nada (You're welcome)." I answer.

The woman looks at me keenly.

"Don't worry about your son. He will be born healthy and grow up to be a wise and good man," she says. Her voice is warm, gentle and calm.

A quick, surprised look at my husband, although he does not understand anything from this conversation. He doesn't speak Spanish yet. How does she know I'm pregnant? First of all, it's only the third month and nothing is visible, and secondly, even if it were visible, I am dressed in a fashionable at that time coat, wide and long, almost reaching the ground. And how does she know I was worried. I didn't say it out loud, but probably like many women expecting a child, especially the first one, I often thought about a healthy birth. I smile at the woman shyly. I am silent.

"You have a lot to do in life. It won't always be easy...But you chose it yourself...You will change the lives of many people, although not everyone will appreciate it...not everyone knows and wants to listen... And jealousy is a powerful tool of evil, to which many people succumb...But angels have a big heart, and they look with the heart...like you...and our hearts sometimes bleed...today not everything will go as you want, but don't worry...our brother will help you...brothers and sisters will always help you when you ask them to do so..."

Dear God! What is this woman talking about? What brother? I don't have any brother...I only have one sister...I feel, however, that what she is saying is something important...But

I'm only 22 years old and I don't know much about life...And now the most important thing is the baby I am carrying under my heart...However, her words make tears appear in my eyes, not knowing why...

"Honey, what is she saying?" asks my concerned husband. "What did she tell you?"

"Nothing much. All is well."

"Buen dia, señora (Good day)" I am addressing the woman.

"Buen dia, hermana... (Have a good day, sister).

My husband takes my hand. We are walking away...

We enter the agency. Last time there was a crowd of people here. Mostly, like us, emigrants. Today it is almost empty. We go to the window. After a short conversation with the clerk, it turns out that we will not receive our benefits today. The rules have just changed. First, we have to turn in our Polish passports to the police, which was not required before, and return with a green card, and this will take a few days. It turns out that many people took advantage of a loophole in the law and collected their benefits using a passport while only passing through or on a tourist trip.

We leave the building and start laughing. Not only do we have no money for food, but even for a train ticket to go home. I will not mention the subway. Well...the only hope is in friends...and the only Poles we know here. At that time, Spain was not a popular destination for Polish emigration. In Madrid and the surrounding area there were maybe 40-50 families. However, the time I am describing was the beginning of a great boom. Already a year later, it was possible to count Poles in thousands.

We can't afford the subway, so there is a long march to the city center. Despite the problem, we are calm and optimistic. As always. The place where the beggar sat a few minutes ago is empty. There is also no sign that anyone was here.

"What did she want from you?"

"Nothing...She said strange things...about angels..."

"Maybe some loca (crazy)?"

"I don't think so...she spoke to me as if I was an angel...and she also said that about herself..."

"The fact that my wife is an angel I know, but this woman looked more like una bruja (witch)."

"Don't say that...Not always everything is like it seems...I wonder how she knew something was going to go wrong today. She said that my brother would help me..."

"But you don't have a brother"

"Well, that's it..."

After about an hour we reach the hostel where my husband's friends live, and now also mine. A young couple of our age who came to Madrid a few months earlier. They knew my husband from Poland. We enter their room. They have a guest. Young, slim, tall, handsome blond. As it turned out later, a neighbor from the second floor. Our friends are visibly overjoyed at the sight of us. We also like to get together with them and although we are completely different, it is always nice, cheerful and loud. After a short polite conversation, we tell them about our problem and ask if they could lend us any money for a few days. At least for tickets back home. Unfortunately, it turns out that our friends are broke, they will get their benefits not sooner than in a week and they are also looking for a loan. And so, a small problem begins to grow into a really big problem. During our conversation, the guy, who never once spoke, leaves tactfully.

An hour passes, and we are still at the starting point, and we still do not really know what to do next. Our friends' room is quite small. It's stuffy. We decide to go out into the fresh air. In the corridor we stop for a moment. We are waiting for our friends who have been approached by the hostel's owner. And while we are waiting in this rather unpleasant, dark corridor, suddenly the newly met blond appears. He comes up to us, gives us a thousand pesetas and says:

"I hope that's enough. You will pay back when you have it."

I often think about that day in Madrid. It was then, for the first time, that I understood the power of empathy and what it means to look with the heart. I've always done it, but I couldn't name it. I thought everyone had that. On that day I realized that while looking with the heart we always, always see more. Angels are everywhere and anyone can be an angel to anyone. Brother and sister. Sometimes angels appear for a very short while. Usually some random meeting, accidental word, gesture, although there is really no such thing as a coincidence. Everything is for something. That day in Madrid, for the first time, I consciously experienced that the good comes back when you least expect it and comes from a completely different direction than you are looking at.

Afterwards we were many times in the agency for benefits, but we had never met that begging woman again. The guy who lent us money also left shortly afterwards. We managed to give it back. A few months after this event, our baby was born. Healthy, although during childbirth there were some complications. It was necessary to administer anesthesia. I was awakened by my husband's voice:

"Honey, we have a beautiful son...such a little angel..."

Freedom

The horse gallops faster and faster through the open space, somewhere in the middle of the Ecuadorian Andes. He knows the area, I don't. However, I have the impression that I have been here before. At another time, in another world, in another reality. Unknown places, but so familiar. I intuitively coordinate my movements with the movements of the animal. Although this is my first horseback riding in this life, I feel like I've always done it. I know exactly how to behave. It's something familiar. Natural. As if a memory of previous lives. The soul is torn apart by a boundless sense of happiness. And this freedom...

Ecuador, "the middle of the world," the end of the eighties. Before I flew to South America, I was fascinated by the books of Erich von Däniken, who had infected me with his concept of extraterrestrial civilizations, who had been visiting our earth for millennia. According to the Swiss, there are plenty of traces of their existence on earth, including the pyramids in Egypt. The most, exactly on the South American continent. Primitive humans of that time saw space travelers as gods. They erected for them temples, statues, cut their images in rocks, built something like airports, and told stories in the range of concepts and vocabulary available to them, as they understood them. It is much easier for people to create a fairy tale accessible to their perception of comprehension and believe in it than to believe in something they do not understand. A great example is Nikola Tesla's remotely controlled boat, which he presented at Madison Square Garden in New York in 1898. Guided by a wireless transmitter the boat accelerated, slowed down and turned in a small pool. However, radio waves are invisible in our range of vision and are rather difficult to imagine. A large part of the spectators gathered at the show preferred to believe that inside this boat sits a tiny man who maneuvers it—because in circuses, various "freaks" could be seen—than to believe in some radio message, or something new and unknown, which they had not dealt with before. So also, our ancestors, having come into contact with something they had not seen before, created their gods. They paid tribute to them and were giving away their freedom.

The human mind is an enormous and often underestimated tool of power. And it's so easy to program. You are either a victim or a winner. No matter the circumstances. Everything is in our head. Because everything that is really valuable in this life we get for free—our body, soul, health, our mind, love, joy, smile, nature, mother earth, singing birds, the sound of trees, people who love us, no matter who we are, and many other things. Paradoxically, however, we value the most what we have to pay for. The more, the more valuable this thing seems. Also, our freedom. And yet everything is in our head. A truly free man, even if he is in bondage, will still remain free in his soul.

So, when, as a very young person, I flew to the southern continent of America, I imagined that here I would have the opportunity to see something extraordinary. To touch the alien civilization, maybe to get to know their descendants…I actually saw and experienced a lot of interesting things, but I didn't meet aliens. But I saw what feudalism looks like in practice—although Ecuador is, after all, a Republic—and I understood what freedom really is.

I am stopping the horse and for a long time enjoy the silence and the beauty of surrounding nature. I feel so free, and joy just bursts inside me. I smile. I don't have to do anything. No one bothers me. There is no one. No distractions. There is only this moment. And there are birds, wind, rustle of trees. In the distance high to the sky, massive peaks of mountains. I don't really know where I am, but I don't care at all. A smile turns into a loud laugh. "Let this moment last!" I shout with all my might. Oh, how good... So good...

"Lead home," I say to the animal and lightly press his body with my legs. I don't know how I know the horse understands me. I just know. We are galloping again. After some time, we reach a familiar route. The horse seems to be reading my mind. We slow down. Now we are riding at walk. There are no buildings. There are only trees behind which expanses of bright-green meadows are stretching. Just around the corner, I unexpectedly come across a Jeep standing on the side of the road. From distance I can see a flat tire. It must have run over some sharp stone. By the open trunk a well, fashionably dressed man looking about sixty years old. The Indian turns around, and a wide smile appears on his face.

"Hola, buenos días, señorita, como esta, usted? (Hello, good morning, lady, how are you?)" He greets me friendly.

"Buenos días," I answer politely, albeit somewhat distrustfully.

"A good day for a horse ride. And good area."

"Yes, you are right. Great ride and a beautiful day."

"I saw a lady from the distance, but I didn't want to interfere. The lady is white, but you can see that she has a free Indian soul. Where did the lady come from?"

"From a distant country. From Poland."

"Poles are free spirits and have pride in their hearts, although also a difficult history. Your hearts are brave and courageous. Just like ours, Indian. You are trusting just like us. You were also betrayed by those whom you had as friends and who took your land from you. But tradition, language and a sense of community have survived. It is the strength of wise tribes. Your strength. And ours."

I already like him...however there is surprise in my head. One of the last things I would expect to find here in the middle of the Andes, almost in the wilderness, is to meet someone who knows my country and my people.

"Do you know Poland?" I ask.

"Yes. I lived in Warsaw for four years while studying."

"I'm also from Warsaw...You speak Polish." I state more than I ask. I say this in my native language.

"Rather I was speaking," he answers in Polish with a hardly audible accent. "I haven't used it for so many years that I forgot."

For a moment we talk about his memories from Poland. I find out what he studied, which dishes he likes, which places he visited and of course I hear, that Polish females are the most beautiful girls in the world and good companions and housewives, just like Indian women.

"Do you live here somewhere in the area? Do you need help? Can I notify someone?" I ask looking at the broken wheel.

"No thanks. I can handle it. I have a spare. I don't live in the area. I'm looking for someone. And I hope to find that person this time."

"And where did you come from, if I may ask?"

"From Guayaquil–the largest city of Ecuador located in its western part and the main port of this country."

"Good luck then. And thank you for the conversation. It was nice to meet you."

"Goodbye lady. Maybe we'll meet again one day. The world is not as big as it seems, and life is unpredictable." He smiles warmly. "And please never lose your freedom."

I ride away. Soon I reach the wide-open gate of the hacienda where I am staying as a guest. A short Indian in a traditional poncho and a hat comes towards me; one of the many who work here. Local Indians often wear hats. Contrary to the generally accepted name, the hats we call "Panama" originally came from Ecuador. Originally, they were hand-woven from plant fibers by local Indians. The name "Panama" was adopted during the construction of the Panama Canal, when this type of hat became popular in the United States.

The Indian smiles at me. I'm white, I have blonde hair, I smile at them, I treat them with respect and I'm curious about a different than mine culture, I keep asking about everything. No wonder that I arouse a lot of curiosity and trust in the local Indians.

"I see that the lady is happy with the ride." He speaks with that strange accent of his own, which even I can hear, although my Spanish still leaves much to be desired. However, this is an accent different from what I have heard among people of Quito. I noticed that some of the employees communicate with each other in their own language, unknown to me.

"Yes. Very." I answer jumping to the ground.

"The horse did not cause trouble?"

"No, he did a great job." I say stroking the animal's neck.

"The lady rides well. Where did the lady learn to ride a horse? In Poland?"

The Indians working here can neither read nor write and rather do not know where this mysterious Poland is and what kind of country it is, but they know that I just came from there. One of the women even asked me: "Señorita, and how many hours by car do you drive to your country?" She was surprised when I replied that by car it would be rather difficult to get there. Maybe she thought it was somewhere in the middle of a tropical jungle. Unfortunately, I did not have time to explain it, because someone interrupted our conversation.

"It was my first time."

"Impossible. The lady likes to joke."

"I'm not kidding."

We head towards the house. And the house is really big. Wooden. On each side, two perpendicular wings are adjacent to it. A veranda was built along the entire front part. The left wing is occupied by workers. I looked there, as if by accident, right after I arrived. The door was wide open. One large room, and on the floor some mattresses or straw paliasses. There was a group of people there older and younger women, some were sewing something, one was feeding a baby, men were sleeping, and in a small free space, almost in silence, several children were playing. At that moment, it was a shock to me. I've never seen people live in such conditions before. And those mute glances of the big little curious eyes in which there was...serenity. A different world. Later I found out that they were mostly people from the jungle. They were not slaves. They volunteered to work on farms most of them belonging to Afro-descendants and mestizos—for food and shelter, sometimes for a meager salary that barely covered their basic needs. The brutal civilization of the West deprived them of their land, polluted the natural environment of their lives and pushed them to the margin. It took away their free world and home.

"Señora asked about the lady. She asked the lady to come to her when she came back from the ride. She's behind the house."

"Thank you." This, natural for me, word "thank you" always raises the surprise of Indian workers. Nobody here thanked them for anything.

I find the pensive middle-aged hostess sitting on the grass on the edge of a cliff rising behind the house. I sit next to her. The woman turns her face to me, smiles and returns to her thoughts again. In silence we look at the range of mountain peaks stretching in front of us reaching the sky. Words are superfluous. We both feel the immensity of beauty given to people by the Creator. Andes. The longest mountain range on earth, stretching along the Pacific Ocean from the gulf of the Caribbean Sea in the north to Tierra del Fuego in the south, over 9,000 kilometers. Mountains with the world's highest volcanoes, which are a kind of gateway to the interior of the earth. Andes, mountains connecting two worlds—heaven and earth.

"I love these mountains," says the woman.

"It's beautiful here."

"Do you see this mountain opposite us?" Saying this, she points with her hand at the slope covered with green grass. "This area belongs to us. Also, that and that one." She indicates the mountain on the right and on the left.

"WOW!"

"We have large herds of cows, and they need to be grazed somewhere." My hostess and her husband are engaged in cattle breeding, from whose milk they make cheese. They also have a lot of horses, serving primarily employees in their daily duties.

"Have you lived in this place for a long time?"

"Since our wedding. We inherited this hacienda from my husband's parents. We expanded, bought land, multiplied the number of cattle, and thus increased the production of milk and cheese."

"Your husband is a good man and very family minded."

"Yes. I couldn't wish for someone better. We raised three daughters and a son together, and we have grandchildren." I'm the guest of one of her daughters.

"And where are you from? From Quito?"

A moment of silence.

"I don't really know. I was born somewhere in the jungle...I spent the first few years in our village, and then everything changed."

"Your parents moved?"

"No. My mother died at my birth. Dad was shot by white people who were looking for new land and cutting down our trees. I only stayed with my older brother."

"Do you remember something from that period?"

"I was tiny. But I remember freedom and our community. We walked around naked. Uninhibited. We were all family to each other, we helped each other, we did everything together. I still have in my ears the melody of those songs that we sang together in the evenings by the fire."

"How did it happen that you left that place?"

"I was five or six years old. My brother went to the river to catch some fish for a meal. I remember that he never let me stray away from the village alone. He left me, as always, playing with other children. But I didn't listen to him that day. I don't know why, and I don't remember why I wandered off. Maybe I ran after a butterfly? I remember those beautiful colorful butterflies...Oh, they were beautiful... Suddenly, I heard a strange noise behind my back...I turned around and saw white people...men... There were several of them...in the village they warned us against whites...I crouched behind a bush...I wanted to hide...but they have already seen me...They laughed and said something among themselves in their own language...then I did not understand, now I know that it was English...They approached...and they just took me...when I started screaming, one of them covered my mouth with his hand and put a knife to my neck...With a gesture, he showed me to be quiet...I cried in silence...Then he threw me on his back ...They walked for some time, stopping several times along the way to rest ...For me, it was an eternity... I was so scared...I still remember that fear...Then we came to some place where I think their camp was. There were horses, tents, and a few other white men. We spent the night there. Then we went on horseback..." Tears appeared in the eyes of my interlocutor. Her voice trembled. It was clear that despite the passage of time, these memories still hurt.

"Why did they take you?"

"They took me to England...and gave to someone as a gift..."

"As a gift?!"

"Yes. I was a gift. They gave me to a married couple as a mascot for their daughter a little older than me..."

"That's terrible..." I feel my anger rise. "Did you live there for a long time?"

"No...they quickly got bored with me...They gave me to someone else...Then someone else and someone else...I've been to a few houses...Apparently I was too wild and too slow...They said that I was disobedient, rude...I was renamed a few times because everyone liked something different...I forgot my name given by my parents...But I haven't forgotten my brother's name...Finally, at the age of ten, I found myself with an older childless couple...They took care of me...They treated me like a daughter and offered love...They also gave me an education...I was able to come to Ecuador to study in Quito. There I met my husband..."

"Have you tried to find your village?"

"Yes. But it was difficult...No one could tell me where I was found, and I didn't remember much myself... I searched for many years, but I never found out...People died, left…in the meantime there was a war... Then I stopped...I had a different life...children, husband, this hacienda...other things were important..." "Buenos dias," we hear suddenly behind our backs. We turn around. The Indian from the broken wheel is heading in our direction. "We are meeting again...I told you," he smiles at me.

"Good morning, again." I answer. "Did you find what you were looking for?"

"It seems so..." he says looking infatuated at my companion. "Yes…I'm sure I did..."

"Buenos dias." The woman's voice is uncertain, unusual for her. I look at her and see a strange excitement on her face. "Who are you? What brings you here?"

At this point, looking straight into her eyes, the man is speaking something in a language unknown to me. She automatically responds, as if unknowingly. However, she immediately reflects and adds in Spanish: "I did not think that I remember anything…The language of my childhood…Who are you?"

"You look exactly like our mom…I've finally found you…Half a century of searching…It paid off…I am your brother…"

We sit in the big living room of the hacienda sipping coffee with milk. In the fireplace, a yellow-red fire dance cheerfully. Previously, the men played on three guitars beautiful local nostalgic music that can be listened to and listened to. Now, the found brother is telling his story.

"We are Eberá Indians. In our language, 'ẽberá' means a local man, an indigenous person. Even in the nineteenth century, Colombia, as well as the areas of today's Panama, were inhabited almost exclusively by the indigenous people of Eberá and Guna…And then the white man came and began to destroy our world. Initially, we treated the whites as gods who had come down to us again from the stars and whom we had long been expecting. We thought they were friends. But they came for our land and our forest. We had to emigrate to other areas. The tribes dispersed. Ours moved near the border with Ecuador. That's where I was born, and then my sister. Our mother died at her birth. Five years later, whites shot our father…in front of my eyes…They came across a group of our men in the forest and wanted to enslave us. We only had bows, they had shotguns. We escaped, but unfortunately, our father had no luck in this skirmish…although we Indians look at matters of death differently than whites. I was fifteen at the time. I was a man. I had to take care of my sister. And one day she just disappeared…Then I found out that someone had seen a group of whites with an Indian girl…But the trail broke off…I only found out that they were English…then the war broke out…But I didn't stop looking…It took me over forty years…And finally I found you, my little sister…" He says this last sentence looking tenderly into her eyes.

"I don't remember much," says the woman. "Flowers in women's hair…Butterflies…singing… melodies…Dad holding me in his arms…I don't remember his face…but I remember you laughing, carrying fish you just caught…And then there was only fear…"

"You were little…and so cheerful, so trusting, so curious…and so independent…you kept laughing and constantly asking questions…you wanted to know everything…you asked me to teach you how to fish… For you, I was a champion…"

One of the guitarists sets the tone and, in a moment, the other two join in. This time the music is accompanied by words. The Spanish language is simply made for singing. No other language sounds as beautiful in songs as Spanish. When they finish, I turn to the man:

"Who are Eberá? What are your roots?"

"Old people tell this story, which has been passed down for generations: In the beginning there was only the sky, the sea and the jungle. Once upon a time, Our Mother Tachi Nawe descended from heaven to earth to live on Baudó Beach by the Choco River. There she gave birth to a son, Our Father, Tachi Ak'õre. The son kept asking his mom where he could meet someone to play with and talk to. He felt lonely. Finally, he said: 'Mom, I'm going to create people.' Tachi Nawe replied: 'That's well son, you will create people. But think first of how you're going to do it.' And so, God Tachi Ak'õre began his work. First, he collected materials needed to prepare puppets that were to transform into living people. He made them of clay and brava reed. The puppets were different, small, big, pretty, ugly...He used different raw materials, that's why we are different...because that's how he created us...When the puppets were ready, he placed them next to him on the beach and at midnight breathed life into them. He told them, 'Get up, because you'll be like me.' When the puppets came to life, Tachi Ak'õre saw that they all had brown skin, so he decided to distinguish them. For this, he created a pond with a brave fish (peces bravos) and ordered his creatures to jump straight into the water one by one before the water dried. Not everyone did it at the same time. Those who jumped in first became white; those who jumped in later got a darker color of mestizos. Eberá jumped when there wasn't a lot of water, so our skin is copper. The last to jump when the pond had already dried up were the Blacks, which is why their skin is the same color as the mud. Finally, depending on the color of their skin, Tachi Ak'ore gave each of his creatures a different language so that they could communicate with it in their own way. And all these languages are known and understood only by Tachi Ak'ore...This is how people, races and languages were born. However, at the beginning of creation, we were all created in the same color and spoke the same language, which is why we are all brothers."

For a long time, everyone is silent.

"It is interesting how in many, completely different cultures, the tales about the creation of man and the purifying power of water converge," I say.

"My Eberá and peoples like us, we have our cosmovision of the world. The worlds of spirit and matter are intertwined. The beings we called gods came from the stars, and people then added their own stories. For us, Eberá, the greatest values are: our nature, tradition, solidarity and reciprocity. And, of course, our freedom. But for you, as a Pole, this is probably very close. You also have your 'Solidarity' and this is not a random name. Only concerted, joint action can defeat the colossus."

"Since I was a child I have felt...in fact I know, that there is something more than this so-called truth that the world is trying to impose on me...When I try to talk about it, about what I feel, how I see...dream... as if the memory of previous lives...people look at me distrustfully...as at an Other...I learned to be silent on this subject...For the first time I meet someone for whom what I feel is something natural...someone who sees the same thing and in the same way..."

"Being different is an honor. Being average is a curse. The world is changed by those who do not fit into mediocrity. They think differently and act differently. Every soul has its own way to proceed in this life. The Creator not only made us different, but also gave us free will. He gave us freedom. Free will means that, regardless of the conditions, or the so-called circumstances of fate, as many call it, it is we who decide how we will live the life given to us. Not making a decision is also a decision."

"But why do children suffer so often?" My hostess made more of a statement than asking a question.

"Dear sister, everything is for something...every suffering helps us to enter the path of destiny...If you were an ordinary average child with a slave nature, you would probably become a slave...a maid in an English house. But you were free... different...they must have said you were naughty...rebellious...you did not fit into the narrow perception and artificial conventions...they didn't want to know you or understand you...they wanted to train you...bring down to your level...It is possible to be in captivity and still remain free. Because Freedom is in our head, heart and soul. Freedom is a state of mind... And this is how our Creator has made us."

Somewhere nearby, the guitar strings sounded again slightly moved with skilled fingers.

Freedom

Passer-By

She slowly heads towards the lifeguards' booth. Her sports shoes leave clear marks on the sand wet at this time. It's early Sunday morning. The beach is almost completely empty. Somewhere in the distance, someone is running, and someone else is playing with their dog. The waves of the ocean lazily come and go. As if casually. Peace, silence, the sound of waves and the cry of birds. Heaven all around, and hell in my head.

Using the low ladder, she skillfully climbs onto a small wooden platform. Puts down the backpack, takes off the jacket, sits on it and rests the back against the booth. She lights a cigarette and looks pensively at the Pacific. Long held in tears run down her cheeks. Not days, not weeks, not months...years...She always had to be so strong. Courageous. Enterprising. Support others and take care of others. She could not afford to be weak. Some adored and admired her, others envied and criticized her. But she rarely noticed how fragile and vulnerable she was inside. A little girl who wanted love so much and for someone to finally take the burden of being responsible for this whole fucked up world off her shoulders. To be hugged and just told "Honey, you've got me. You don't have to carry it yourself anymore. I am here. Let me take care of you. Rest and smile at me." It's just that little girls usually have loving dads who treat them like little princesses. And she didn't even experience it. The heroine of the family... Always brave, courageous, responsible...And now?... Now it turns out that what she had believed to be the truth for fifty years had collapsed like a house of cards. For what is truth? Delusion. It is nothing else but what someone wants to believe. Everyone has a lot of fairy tales, on various topics, which they consider to be the only, legitimate truth. And is ready to fight for that fairy tale truth and kill anyone who disagrees with it. It hurts when confrontation comes, and Fate pulls the dark blindfold off the eyes. When it turns out that the fairy tale truth is just plain shit truth, and everything that has been so far and seemed solid was actually based on fragile clay legs.

Somewhere above her head, she hears the joyful mewing of the seagulls. She looks at the nearby pier digging into the ocean. A scene appears before his eyes: she goes to the end of the pier, climbs the barrier and jumps. Plunges into the abyss and never swims out again. And finally, it's the end...But the end of what? Earthly concerns? Death is only liberation from the material shell, and yet consciousness lives on, only in a different form and dimension. And you can no longer change or fix anything. Death ends nothing.

From a small pocket of the backpack, she takes out a special sachet ashtray, into which she puts the cigarette butt.

Looks at the water for a moment, listening to the rhythmic sound of the waves, and then closes her eyes. The cheeks are still wet, and the tears do not stop flowing. She looks up at the sky. "Where are you who calls yourself God and whom I called Dad? And do you exist at all? A God who does not exist...If a Father, a good daddy, and he lets his children suffer...Why are you testing me so much?! All my life you don't do anything, you just punch...Who are you?! ...Because you're certainly not goodness...You're playing with human life... You take away ones dreams...You hold that fucking joystick and play with human life...Do you have fun? It's not enough yet?... You check how much someone can endure?.Listen, you up there...I've had enough! Do you hear?! I'm tired of your games...I don't want such a Father, and I don't want you to exist...Once I wanted...I believed that everything was for something and there is your justice...but it's all shit...there is no justice...Evil wins and laughs in everyone's face...Shitty Matrix created by and for boys that someone once called gods...But it's all just a fucking illusion...a daydream...Your...Your game...But you know what? People have feelings...And the more sensitive and honest they are, the more they suffer...What, you forgot? Or maybe you didn't know at all?... The error of creation...You didn't foresee...you wanted to create a being in your image and likeness, and something did not work out...Unintentionally, feelings appeared in this being...And suffering...And now you're playing with those feelings...and you check..." The anger that shook her makes silent tears turn into loud crying. She looks up at the sky and almost screams "Stop! Do you hear?! Stop playing with my life anymore! Stop testing me. I don't want to...I've had enough!...

Do something good for a change...Just help..." These last words she says quietly...Almost in a whisper...She lowers her head, hugs her knees with her hands, and huddled cries.

She herself does not know how long she lasts in such a state of non-being. Tears flow and flow...And she doesn't even try to stop them. And again, there is this feeling of longing for another world. Not this earthly world, but another one. In a different reality, dimension, time. Once again, she feels that she does not belong here, that she was here by mistake...or by the stupid whim of some boy-god who decided to have fun at her expense.

Suddenly she feels someone's presence. She lifts her tearful face and sees a standing athletic, fair-haired middle-aged man smiling at her amicably.

"You don't mind if I sit next to you for a moment and look at the world from your perspective." This is rather a statement than a question. And before she could answer, the man skillfully climbs the ladder and sits next to her. She quickly wipes away the tears. Tries to calm down.

For a while they sit in silence and observe the calm surface of the ocean. The man doesn't seem to notice her tears. The woman hopes that he will leave quickly, and she will be able to return to her thoughts again. After a while, however, she realizes that his presence does not bother her at all. Well! This presence seems to be soothing. It makes her feel inner peace. Bad thoughts flew away somewhere and followed the seagull's mewing...Or maybe they just hid for a moment only to later strike with double force? She grasps this moment...this moment of blissful peace and security.

"The ocean is like the insides of a human being." The man suddenly speaks softly. "Sometimes it is good and calm, and sometimes it is angry and turbulent." He interrupts. A moment of reflection. After a while, however, he continues. "Few people notice that the ocean is life and gives life itself. Its duration are constant emotions. Laborious overcoming of rock obstacles...the fight with the wind...but also for some time, the fight with man. However, ocean always wins. Do you know why? Not because it's enormous. Because it is persistent. True to itself. And although it is a loner, it is a warrior. And all that lives in it are warriors."

"The ocean a warrior? I've never looked at it that way."

"Not you alone. People think they are the masters of this world...but they are just ordinary passers-by... They do not see the spirit of nature. They fail to see that the earth is alive...Breathes...it is a separate entity, only in a form other than human. They do not respect what they have received as a gift."

"And what is life?... A form of captivity. Everyone is a slave of someone or something...thoughts, cravings, objects, money...a slave of some god... If you want to be free, they try to break you...throw restrictions into your box. You become an outsider...Different...Unwanted...And if people don't do it, those so-called gods who threw us into this Matrix and have a lot of fun will do it...How do we know we're not their toy?... the toy of the one we call God... How do we know that this whole life is not a daydream...a computer game of someone up there...and the only goal is to break you...your psyche... what's the point of all this?"

"Maybe it's like you say, or maybe it's not...People have created many lies and fairy tales in which they themselves believed...Religion is also a fairy tale. God is a fairy tale. And every religion is a sect. Its sole purpose is power over the hearts, minds, and souls of people. And driving people into guilt...Sin... confusing people in their heads...Distracting from nature and the true essence of life...The eternal question of philosophers—did god create man or man god?" Anger can be heard in her voice.

"But people like fairy tales. They want to live in a fairy tale, and they want to believe in their fairy tales. They give them a sense of security, simplify and organize.' the man answers gently.

"However, life is something more than that. People reduce it to material matters...and yet in reality it's all about spirituality. About learning to love...yourself and others...balance and inner peace..."

"Look at the ocean. Calm, gentle, friendly and beautiful. And so, it is most of the time. But it can also be threatening and turbulent. It is inscrutable like the soul of a human being. Sometimes it is torn by storms. But the storms pass, and it lasts. The storm is on the surface, caused by wind, rain. But the deeper, the calmer. The soul is tranquility, and it is the Ego of man that creates the storms."

The woman is silent. It is surprising that this strange man says what she also feels and subconsciously knows forever.

"There is a Buddhist story about a certain ring," the man continues. "Well, there was once a young emperor who could not cope with difficulties. When things were going well in the state, the emperor rejoiced and celebrated beyond measure. He thought it would always be like that...that he has conquered and reigns over everything, for he is the master of this world...the master of life and death... He forgot that everything in life is changing... And when a difficult time came, the emperor became very angry. He did not want to learn from this experience...blamed everyone around...he did not see at all that his decisions led to such a situation...he asked his advisers what to do. He was expecting answers, but he wasn't really listening to them at all...And they were afraid to say something, because they could easily lose their heads if something they said did not, please the emperor. They were considered enemies. Eventually, the advisors came up with an idea. They gave the emperor a ring and said, 'This ring is magical. It contains the answer to all your questions, Lord.' Astonished but also curious, the emperor took the ring and stared it. It was a simple wedding ring without any ornaments or stones. Inside was an engraved inscription: 'This will also pass'...From then on, when it was bad, the emperor was no longer angry. He already knew that whatever happened, whether good or bad, everything did not last forever...because it would also pass...and something new will come..." The man interrupts for a moment, and then looking the woman straight in the eye, he says. "Whatever happened to you, remember that it will also pass..."

"It has already passed...but it has left a deep mark...And big wounds...And it's so hard to deal with them...It's so hard to deal with the past."

"Your past no longer belongs to you?"

"How is it not mine? After all, this is my past. And my past has an impact on me today."

"You can't change it. But it is you who decides what you will take from it."

"Only that this past comes back like a boomerang."

"Someone hurt you," the fair-haired interlocutor does not ask, but states the fact. He knows.

"Yes." The woman answers after a short hesitation.

"The man you loved."

"All the men I loved. But this one the most. I still love him...He also loves me...He is afraid of love...Like my father..."

"And you?... You don't run away from love?"

The woman is silent for a moment.

"I think so..." She says with hesitation in her voice, "Yes...I want to love, and yet I am afraid of love...I leave first to feel in control."

"You run away."

"I think so...yes, I'm running away..."

"Why?"

"Because He up there takes away from me everyone I love... Love hurts."

"He doesn't take anything away from you...And love gives happiness."

"For a moment...and then there is only pain..."

"Tell me about your father..."

"Dad..." pensivity in the voice, "the guy who determined my whole life. Each of my partners was similar to him in some way. Everyone was different, but everyone was equally immature. With each of them I had to rework some version of my father..."

"How did you remember him?"

"He was free...He was a really free guy. Idealist...As if out of this world...He loved life, nature, people... He did not attach himself to matter...He laughed a lot and turned everything into a joke. He was able to find something positive in everything. He enjoyed seemingly tiny things. I used to not understand that. Now I see that I am like that myself. I watch the flower grow and my heart rejoices. He was just like that...I used to think that he was also a damn egoist and thought only about himself...but that's not true...someone told me this ...mom...he shared everything and was able to give everything to others... He was good...He just lived in the here and now and enjoyed every moment..."

"And how did you remember him as a child?"

"The best dad in the world." She answers without thinking. "I don't remember my mother from my childhood at all, but there was always my dad. He bathed me, read bedtime stories, took me to the children's theater, to the cinema for matinees, cooked for me and with me, went to church with me, sang, went to parent teacher meetings, visited me at camps, and even brought sandwiches to school when I forgot...Every year before Christmas, he made paper stars and Christmas tree chains with me...It was my dad who instilled in me love for books and for learning. He kept saying that I was smart, and he believed in me. He always treated me like an adult. I felt that he was proud of me...And when I did something that others condemned, he said that apparently, I had my reasons to make such a decision... We talked a lot...It was always fun with him...And when I was an adult, he always asked me for opinions. Especially in matters of politics..." The woman smiles at her thoughts.

"It looks like you had a great father. Not everyone is so lucky."

"Unfortunately, there was also this dark side. Immaturity, irresponsibility, Peter Pan mentality and alcohol, constant quarrels with mom...Screams...I was running away...I was afraid...Although alcohol came later...And after alcohol, he could be aggressive and vulgar...But never toward me...He never hit me...And he never yelled at me...No, none of these things...He just cursed more...It was because of alcohol that I backed away from him. I've also never attracted a guy who is prone to alcohol in my adult life...Maybe it's because I set such boundaries for my father...I said that I would not tolerate his behavior and if he wanted to talk to me only when sober...My father was appearing and disappearing...And I was waiting...Emotional swing....It took a long time for us to start talking again...Several years...I have the impression that he felt ashamed and probably afraid of me...He was afraid that I would discover how weak he was...Or maybe he just respected?...He did not dare to call me or meet me when he had a glass cup..." The woman is pensively silent for a moment. "When I think about it now, I just realized that he was afraid that I would reject him...He was afraid of rejection. Yes...My father was afraid of rejection..." She repeats it slowly, emphatically, as if surprised, as if she had just understood something very important. For a moment she sinks into her thoughts, and the absent sight reveals that her consciousness is somewhere else entirely.

"The ebbs and flows of the ocean...Happy you touch the waves, and they suddenly recede...That's why you ran away from love? You were also afraid of rejection."

"I think so...Yes."

"But when you dare to go in further, deeper, you no longer feel the ebb tide. There are only pleasant, gentle waves surrounding you from every side. And you don't want to run away anymore. And so it is with good love."

"Maybe you're right...or maybe not...In my last relationship, I let myself be carried away by love. I resisted for a long time, but I finally opened up. I stopped controlling and running away. I entered this ocean of love. And you know what? I have never known so much happiness in my life. I was drunk with this happiness."

"And the man?"

"Him too. He was happy and loving. Only this time, it was he who was scared of love. Because he couldn't control. He withdrew and ran away."

"He wasn't ready. But if he really loved, he will come back. Men do not forget. It's just that sometimes they need more time to understand something."

"Well, I don't know...three months later he married another woman he met after our breakup. And now he can control everything again."

"This woman is just another passer-by in his life. Apparently, he has to experience something, understand something else. It is necessary to give time and trust in the wisdom of the Universe."

"No. It was that Daddy up there who played with my life again. And he's probably laughing now with joy because he won another game of his." Anger is rising in the woman's voice again.

"It doesn't work that way."

"How do you know? He's taking all of them away from me. Everyone I loved. He even took my father away from me."

"He did not take him. He gave."

"Really?" Sarcasm is all too palpable. "I'll tell you something...Speaking of my father, I should have said, 'I once had a father.' He was what he was, but he was. At first, I loved him, then I didn't talk to him for years, I was ashamed of him and I was annoyed by his lifestyle, and then I learned to understand and accept him. We were friends...I loved him...He was one of the closest people to me... and maybe even the closest one...A few days ago, completely unexpectedly...suddenly...I understood something... something has reached me... it was a piece of information I heard in a movie...The funny thing is that I knew about it before, but I never took it personally...I just didn't think about it...I didn't give it a thought...It's as if I'm not letting this thought come to me. Like a blockage of my subconscious. And now...now I don't understand anything, and I feel confused...I am asking—why? Why did someone play with my life so perfidiously?... And in total I paid a high price...I paid with my own life..." Tears begin to flow from the woman's eyes, but the man does not seem to see them.

"What information?"

"My father had blood type '0'...I have 'AB'...a father with blood type '0' cannot have a child with blood type 'AB'...My father was not my father...The man I considered my father for fifty years was not my father." With the last sentence, the woman's voice completely breaks down. She bows her head down, and salty drops as big as peas fall from above on the dry boards of the platform.

"And yet he was," says the interlocutor quietly.

"Everything was a lie. Everything is a lie. This whole world is one big lie. One big shit fairy tale."

"Why don't you want to trust?"

"Trust? Who should I trust? Everyone I trusted left and hurt me. They smashed daggers into my heart and left wounds that do not want to heal."

"Trust the wisdom of the universe. These scars are your strength and wisdom."

"These scars are my prison."

"If you allow the pain of the past seep into your future, you will always be a prisoner of the past. Do you really want to be a prisoner of the past? It's your choice. However, you won't find peace if you're still stuck in the past."

"But that past is still in me. It keeps coming back. It is still manifesting itself."

"Problems and experiences from the past are only hard as long as you keep them. Forgive. If you let go of everything that belongs to the past, then you will be able to enjoy the present moment."

"That's what I told the man who left me."

"Then why don't you do it yourself?"

"And how would you feel if you found out that your father wasn't your father?"

"But he was your father."

"Ok...he raised me...But he was actually a stranger."

"Really a stranger?" The man smiles gently.

"Just a few minutes ago, you told me about the greatest father in the world. About a father who, despite his weaknesses, loved you with an unconditional, absolute love, supported, respected and was proud of you. You also told me about a man who, although he left you because he wasn't ready for your relationship, loved you and gave you a lot of happiness that you hadn't experienced before. Thanks to your father, you are who you are today. A beautiful wise woman, with a wonderful soul. Thanks to this man, you know what love tastes like. You entered the ocean and felt its warmth and beauty. See how many great photos you've accumulated in the album you have in your head. Look at the ocean. People throw tons of garbage into it. And it throws them away and leaves only what he wants to leave behind. And that's why it's beautiful."

The woman is pensively silent.

"But what to do with the pain?" She asks after a while in a calm voice. "And what to do so that what was will not happen again?"

"Forgive and let go. People look back at what they lost, not what they had. You have to look at what you have had, not what you have lost. How do you know what your biological father would be like? Or maybe you just got the best father 'the one up there', as you call him, chose for you? Maybe the man you love was supposed to show you what love is and open you to something even better that will come soon when you're ready. To show you that you should not be afraid of love. You have a beautiful album of memories and stick to it. Protect it and look there as often as possible. Cherish good memories."

The woman is silent. She is already calm. She looks at the lazy ocean and plunges into her thoughts. Smiles.

"People are just passers-by in our lives." She hears the man's voice. "Our partners, acquaintances, strangers, even our parents and siblings. They stay longer or shorter, sometimes they appear for a short while. Each of them has a different role to fulfill. Each of them has to teach us something, show us something, can indicate the direction. We often get angry with those who we think have done us something wrong, hurt us. And yet they only helped us to grow, to experience something, to understand something. The soul is free. We decide what emotions we let into our lives. Often our anger at someone, is anger at ourselves. At something we can't, or rather don't want to deal with...because we don't want to understand. Learn something...Anger and aggression often stem from fear. We decide who we let into our lives. If you're worried about the past, you can't focus on the present and the present moment. Live in the here and now. And thank all those passers-by for wanting to be a part of your life, if only for a brief moment. Live, love and be happy. This is the meaning of life."

After these words, the man gets up and skillfully goes down the stairs jumping on the sand.

"Are you already going?" Asks the woman.

"It's time."

"Who are you? What's your name?"

"Let's say I'm just a passer-by." The fair-haired man smiles peevishly.

"Thank you...thank you for wanting to be a part of my life, albeit for a brief moment, Passer-by."

The woman calmly watches as the fair-haired man walks away slowly. A dog runs up to him and happily wags his tail and jumps around his legs and he begins to caress him affectionately. Her gaze wanders towards the ocean disappearing beyond the horizon. After a while she looks up to the sky. Smiles.

"Thank you...thank you that you are here…Dad..."

Small Gesture

Late Saturday afternoon. Or maybe early evening. It's dark outside, although it's not that late. I've been on the road since morning. From meeting to meeting. I'm off the highway. I stop at the traffic lights. Through the open window I see a begging homeless man. An older, sloppily dressed gentleman. Next to him lie on the ground some packages with his modest belongings, a small folding fishing chair without a backrest and a cardboard plate with the inscription—HOMELESS VETERAN.

A picture like many, here in Southern California. It is estimated that in Los Angeles alone there are about 8 thousand homeless veterans, and in San Diego more than a thousand. There are about 50,000 of them in the entire United States. The majority right here in California (over 12 thousand). They are not dangerous. Rather reconciled with their fate. With a lot of humility in them. Sometimes, when you start talking to them, you hear things that make tears come to your eyes. And you start to wonder...think...to look into oneself...Oh, such simple life wisdom based on experience and not always gracious life.

Without thinking, with a quick, decisive movement, I open the glove compartment in the car. I reach for all the snacks I took with me in the morning, knowing that I would not have time for a meal. I wanted to eat them in a while, because my stomach rumbled like a military band, but it didn't matter anymore. "Excuse me, Sir..." The man turns around and in silence, looks at me questioningly. "Please take it." I give him a banana, an apple, tangerines, homemade sandwiches, some crackers and Chobani cheese packed in a bag with a napkin and a disposable spoon. I also hand him a bottle of extra water, which I always carry in the car.

"Thank you very much... God bless you," he says looking at what he got.

"And you too."

"That's your lunch," he says to me surprised.

"That's OK. Maybe God wanted me to bring it to you." I'm smiling.

The man looked at me with wise, piercing eyes.

"You know, people usually give money, Mc Donald's sandwiches, or leftovers of their meal that they took in a box from a restaurant. They try to silence their conscience and feel better in their own eyes. And you gave something from the heart, spontaneously. This is called Love. Now you will be hungry because you gave me your meal." Saying this, he extends his hand in my direction with the meal he has just received, as if he wanted to return it. I shake my head in a gesture of refusal. "This is the love that Jesus taught, and which people locked up in various churches and religions do not understand," says the man thoughtfully. "I'm not going to tell you 'God bless you' anymore, because you've already found God and understood His teaching...Have a nice evening and thank you." Still looking into my eyes with his piercing gaze, he smiled gently, but somehow warmly.

I hear a car honking behind me. I didn't notice when the light changed from red to green. I smile at the man, wave my hand, and drive away in my direction. I feel a tear run down my cheek…

One Day

There is one day in my life that, despite the passage of many, many years, has firmly sunk into my memory. I was a teenager at the time, but it still feels like it was yesterday.

Sunday morning. I'm at home only with my sister, who is two years younger. We lived in one of the towns near Warsaw. My mother worked on the other side of Warsaw, where she ran a restaurant. The previous day she had organized a wedding and did not return for the night. Dad didn't live with us anymore. My sister and I were alone. My sister was still asleep.

As usual on Sunday morning I turned on the TV to watch a youth program, which was supposed to start at 9:00 a.m. Then I was to go to church for a youth mass. I looked at the screen and saw General Jaruzelski speaking. He had glasses on and was in uniform. I didn't listen to what he was saying. His words seemed to fly past my ears. I switched to the second channel... Nothing...I returned to "one" again...again to "two"...To tell the truth, I thought that the TV had broken down...again "one"...This time, all the time standing in front of the TV, I began to listen...Spoken slowly in a pathetic tone, the words began to reach my consciousness...

"Citizens of the Polish People's Republic! Today I am addressing you as a soldier and as the head of the Polish Government. I turn to you on matters of the utmost importance. Our homeland is at an abyss. Our Polish home, the achievement of many generations, erected from ashes, is becoming a ruin. The structures of the state are ceasing to work..."

I remember that at this point my entire body started to shake. My throat was squeezed tight as if someone had put an entire apple in it.

"Enormous is the burden of responsibility that has fallen on me in this dramatic moment of Polish history. It is my duty to take on this responsibility—it is about the future of Poland, for which my generation fought on all fronts of the war and to which it gave the best years of its life. I announce that today the Military Council of National Salvation has been constituted. TODAY AT MIDNIGHT THE STATE COUNCIL, IN ACCORDANCE WITH THE PROVISIONS OF THE CONSTITUTION, IMPOSED MARTIAL LAW THROUGHOUT THE ENTIRE COUNTRY!."

Tears flowed from my eyes. I was scared. God how scared I was then...There was only one word in my ears—

WAR...Even now, when I write about this event, those emotions come back as if it was happening now, today...Before my eyes I saw the war...And this crazy stream of thoughts...God! What are we going to do now? What will we eat? How will we survive? What will happen when the Russians come...or maybe Germans again?... My imagination produced the most terrible scenes from the conflagration of war. My entire generation was raised on war ethos. Movies, readings, stories...and even everyday life. Although we were born many years after the war, we could feel it, we knew everything about it...and we were very afraid.

I rushed to the phone hanging in the hallway to call my mother. Silence. No signal...God, what will happen now? And if they killed her? After all, it's WAR...Only this word was drilled into my head...

I went back to the room. I stood like paralyzed in front of that TV. I was shaking and crying all the time. I listened to this speech probably ten times. And the longer I listened, the more I was afraid...

After about an hour, my mother arrived. She was very scared. To get home, she had to drive through the whole city. She talked about tanks, soldiers and militia...Then she said that no one knows what will happen, and she has to work, so I should know about some things, and... she showed me all the places in which she hid her savings…To tell the truth, I would have not invented such hiding places in my life...

Then it was as it was. They turned on the phone the next day. Apparently, someone there in the phone switch headquarters in my town, did it by mistake, and because the switch was mega outdated, something did not work, and they could not turn it off again. How much truth there was to this story, I do not know, but the fact is that while Warsaw had its phones turned off, we, in our area, could use them freely. Well, maybe not so freely, because soon we also heard in the handset "controlled conversation" ... But this fear of the first day will probably be with me for the rest of my life. Because never before or since, have I been so afraid as I was then, on December 13, 1981.

Paradoxically, some time later it turned out, that this first day fear, gave Poles strength to fight for their freedom and change the map of Europe. Then others followed us.

One Day

A Tree

A tree was growing. Beautiful, green, healthy, strong. Free. I liked to look at it. I liked to sit under it. I liked to cuddle with it. I liked its calm. It was like me. Independent, free, happy. And although rooted in the ground, This Tree was like a bird. It flew in the skies carried by a gust of wind and was reaching the sky. It was reaching the stars.

And one day the man decided that the tree had too many branches, that it is bothersome, that these branches should be trimmed. And I watched as another man cruelly and brutally cut these branches with a mechanical saw. Like tears the branches fell with a bang to the ground. And tears of silence flowed down my cheeks. I felt the pain of that tree. And I felt its silent scream. My heart was gripped by the pain of severed wings and freedom taken away. I felt unity with this tree. I was that tree. The pain of that tree was my physical and mental pain. I stood, watched in silence, cried in silence and in silence I suffered.

And my daughter came. And she started crying too. And she says, "Mom, this tree is suffering. I feel it. It cries. My heart hurts. Why are they doing this?"

I hugged her in silence. Because how to explain to a child that the Ego of man who wants to control everything destroys the beauty of Life given by the Creator. He takes away Freedom and locks it in cramped cages of Mind Control and Bondage. Reduces to the role of a backyard hen staring at the ground and pecking its worms. Living in the illusion of being an eagle. How to explain to a child that the Arrogance and Pride of man reject and destroy what is most beautiful in him—Absolute Love.

The Creator gave man a choice–Heaven or Hell, Death or Life, Good or Evil. And he showed what Heaven, Life and Good are. Because this is Absolute Love. For everything and for everyone. And everything is One. Absolute Love is Freedom and Acceptance. But also, Humility and Gratitude. And it's all in the heart, not in the head. The Heart is the Soul. The head is a cold computer processing data. But some have forgotten about it. And they are still wrestling with the Father. They put themselves above Him. They try to outwit. Control. They calculate. Share. They judge. They take away Freedom. They clip the wings of others. And they inflict pain...to others, but also to themselves. Because they don't live their lives. Not the life that the Father chose for them to simply be happy. They reject the Gift of Love. They choose Darkness. They become living dead. Like this beautiful tree, of which someone decided to take away its freedom, strength, beauty and light.

However, the Tree will be reborn someday. Because it is strong and free with its freedom. It knows no control and neither hatred. It loves. And it just exists. Man, who has chosen Darkness, Control, and Wrestling with the Creator will never see the true light. He will never taste true Freedom. He will never experience what inner peace and the feeling of boundless Love is. He will not understand what True Happiness really is. Forever he will remain a backyard chicken from the chicken coop, pecking its worms under a beautiful, free Tree. A hen, listening to the crowing of a rooster and dreaming an eagle's dream. But the hen will never soar high. It will never sit on a branch of this Tree. And it will never fly to the stars. It will never know what true Freedom is.

The tree will grow back one day. One day the hen will lose its head, which some other man will decide to cut off with one cut. Because he decided so. Only over the hen, no one will cry. She will be eaten for dinner. And the Tree, will grow further up, will give birth to new green leaves, play together with the wind with its beautiful humming music, and give shelter and shade. And it will share its soothing peace, so different from the chicken's cackling and racket. It will share its Silence, in which a person will rest and hear herself.

Two Mirrors

It is said that the eyes are the window of the soul. And looking into someone's eyes, you can see a real person. You can look into her soul. Because eyes, like the heart, do not lie. But it happens that looking into someone's eyes, you can see yourself there. Reflection in someone's eyes like in a mirror. See your light and your shadow there. It is then said that two twin flames have just met. One soul in two bodies. Two halves of the same apple.

And it happened that a friend gave me two old, perhaps older than me, identical mirrors. They were in poor condition, although beautiful. It was clear that they had gone through a lot, had seen many stories and served many eyes. I accepted the gift with gratitude and decided to restore them to their former glory. Rejuvenate them. First, I took care of the first mirror. I took off the frame, cleaned it with sandpaper, painted it, replaced the board on the back. My son hung it on the wall. The second mirror stood forgotten behind the couch for a year. Until one day I felt that it was time to rejuvenate it, as well. I cleaned the frame so hard and with such enthusiasm that my hands hurt. But I did it. And I was proud of my work. They now hang on two adjacent walls, and one reflects the other. Like two twin flames. Like two halves of an apple. And happy, they tell each other their stories, enjoying being together.

A mirror is something magical. It's like a gateway to another world. You look into it every day. But do you really see the real you in it, or just someone you want to see? Do you see the real you or an actor? The character you play? Look into your eyes and feel what you saw in them. Light or Darkness? Truth or Distortion?

Glass of Water

You reach the wall. The pain is unbearable. You feel that if you don't do something, you'll explode. Everything that is hidden from the world boils inside you. Uncontrollable tears flow down the cheeks spontaneously. You're screaming "God, how much more!!! Why are you doing this to me again?!!! Why don't you love me?!!! Why me again?!!!"

You reach for wine and do something you don't usually do. Although you know well that alcohol is not the answer. Nor a solution. However, you feel that you want it, you need it. You know, too, that alcohol allows you to open up. Throw away all that aching shit. And it doesn't matter if someone really listens or does it out of politeness, and whether they understand what you're saying. The main thing is that by speaking, you begin to feel freed. As if you were throwing tons of dirty debris from your heart. Speaking loud and honest, you're actually starting to talk to yourself. Despite drinking alcohol, something begins to clarify, you start to look at things differently. The legs get tangled, the tongue tangles, the eyes see double and even quadruple. And still those tears.

Someone took care of you. He takes you for a walk to the ocean at night. You look into the tempting black abyss of water and want to immerse yourself in it. Forever. Then someone forces you to eat a hot, spicy Mexican soup. He takes you to an apartment. He puts you in a bed in a separate room. Places a glass of water on the cabinet and allows you to fall asleep. Understands.

You wake up at night. Silence all around. The head begins to hurt. You are thirsty. You reach for the water standing next to you and think warmly about the person who left it there for you. Intrusive thoughts come back. And those tears again. And thoughts. Just before dawn, you fall asleep for a while. Then there are tears again. But in solitude. When no one can see anymore. Thoughts begin to take a different shape. And suddenly you realize that with every flowing tear it's kind of lighter. Peace comes slowly. Understanding. The pain passes. The blessing of Catharsis.

Friend

And it happened that a friend lived in the branches of a tree next to my terrace. A beautiful bird with a wonderful voice, who day and night sang his joyful stories flowing from the heart and sung with the heart. He talked about life, about the soul, about love, about what is on earth and in heaven. He always accompanied me when a smile on my face was present and when melancholy sometimes came, dispelling it with his joyful trebles. And I wrote poems and my fairy tales about life. I called this singer my friend. And so, we complemented each other like secret lovers. He sang and I poured his songs on paper. Or maybe he was the one singing what I was writing.

However, one day my friend fell silent. Disappeared. And it got quiet and as if sad without his beautiful music. The trees continued to dance with the wind like a pair of lovers in a loving embrace. Squirrels jumped nimbly from branch to branch, outdoing each other in this game. Sometimes a v-formation of wild geese flew high in the sky. The leaves yellowed and new, light green appeared. The day became longer, then shorter, and then longer again. I continued to write poems and fairy tales about life, but differently. The singing of love and joy of my winged companion was missing. His smile was missing, which he sprinkled on his every song. I've often thought about him this year. "To whom are you singing now, my friend?" And are you well where you are?

And one day I saw him again in the tree branches. The friend returned home. Tired of the journey, but happy. It was clear that he had gone through a lot, but he regained his freedom. And he regained his voice. And he came back as if more grown-up. At first, his singing was shy. It was as if he was wondering if I would want to listen to the stories, he wanted to sing to me so badly. He talked about pain, longing, love. About what is in the soul and about what is in the grass. About what is on earth and in heaven. However, with each passing day his voice became stronger, more confident, and the songs more and more joyful, but also more mature.

And he stayed that way with me and near me. I write what he sings, and he sings about what I write. And this is our friendship. Based on freedom. Because sometimes you have to fly away to another tree to understand where your home and happiness really are. And the green-leaved branches, on which playful squirrels jump, dance joyfully their beautiful dance of love, in an embrace with the warm wind.

Friend

83

Returning Home

And it happens in life that one day you look around you and think: What am I doing here? I lack air, space. As if someone was clipping my wings. And I cannot spread them out. I am among people who, instead of supporting me, backstab me and pull me down. Seemingly I call them friends, but are they really friends? And all these conversations about nothing. I do different things I don't even like. As if it wasn't mine. As if it wasn't my world. And my soul rushes to something different, more beautiful, more wonderful. But where is my home?

Hello Ugly Duckling! You've just found yourself in your backyard. And even though you're a royal bird, you dig worms out of the ground along with other chickens and try to cackle like them, even though it's not your language. Instead of swimming on a beautiful clean pond in the royal garden, you dabble in a gossipy, narrow-minded mud. Instead of soaring high into the sky, you fly to the height of a chicken fence. Instead of cuddling with love to the royal birds, you listen to the crowing of arrogant roosters. And what will you do with it, Duckling? Maybe it's time to remember who you are, beautiful royal child? It's time to see yourself in the crystalline surface of the lake of your soul. It's time to see your own beauty. Maybe it's time to leave that dirty yard that isn't your world? Maybe it's time to spread your beautiful wings and soar high, high. Reach the sky. Reach for your dreams. All you have to do is reach out. What will you do, Duckling?

"I'm flying. Yes, I already know who I am." It wasn't my world. It wasn't my costume. It wasn't my pond. It wasn't my life. I'm flying. I spread my huge, beautiful, white wings. I'm flying. I'm flying high. Higher and higher. And above. To the top. How wonderful is the world from this height. You can see so differently. More. And so many brothers and sisters who love me and support me here. How good it is to be yourself. How good it is to be in your place. How good it is to be in your palace. I returned home. Thank you.

The Cure

"**I**'m dying," the girl said to the boy.
The boy was silent. His face was cold and unmoved. Tears came to the girl's eyes.

"He's a monster," she thought sadly, and in her mind, she lovingly hugged the monster to her heart.

"I am a monster," he thought, and in his heavy heart he felt a painful prick.

The girl looked into his eyes. There she saw Sorrow, Pain and Fear. But when she looked even deeper, she saw Love.

"Take care of yourself," the girl said with concern, placing her hand on his cheek. "Be healthy."   She turned and began to go into her world.

The boy looked after her unmoved. As if something had chained him to the ground in the place where he stood. Fear. Suddenly, a tear appeared in his eye, which began to flow slowly down his cheek. The boy felt its warmth, which began to penetrate his entire body. But he didn't want to cry. He blinked his eyes and ... He felt like he had just woken up.

Surprised, he looked around him and saw Darkness. He looked after the departing girl and saw Light there. A thorn in his heart creaked and the boy felt a piercing pain in his chest. Intuitively, he began to run in the direction where the girl had gone.

"Wait," he shouted, "I know the cure."

The girl turned around. Calmly, with eyes full of love and acceptance, she looked at the boy. "I love you," he said, looking into her eyes. The thorn in the heart fell to the ground and disappeared. The pain was also gone. The boy caught a deep breath and felt Joy penetrating him. And he understood what Freedom is. He took the girl by her hand and so they walked together in Love towards the Light. The Darkness behind them began to dissolve like Fog until it disappeared completely. And everywhere there was only Love. And the bright Sun smiled from above and illuminated their way.

The World Stopped

And God created all the stars, planets and the entire Universe. And when he had arranged all this according to his plan, God separated Light from Darkness. And then he chose one planet, breathed life into it and illuminated it with a special light. During the day he gave it sunlight, and at night moonlight. And he created water on it—clean rivers, crystalline lakes, seas, and oceans. He also created mountains, forests and all the beautiful vegetation. And on the fourth and fifth days, God filled water, land, and skies with all creations. And God saw that it was good. And he said to the planet, "From now on you will bear the name Gaia, and you will be the mother of all life." And God gave Gaia the power of fertility. And God marveled at his work. Behold, he created Paradise. And then God decided to create man—male and female, as equals—and then gave them this beautiful Paradise. And the Creator said, "Take care of Gaia, and she will repay you richly. You will never lack anything. Love each other, respect each other, live in harmony, health, procreate and be happy.

Man, however, did not listen to the voice of the Creator. He thought he could be more powerful than God and could be a god himself. And man forgot about what was important. And he did not respect the gifts offered to him. Wars for material goods and power began. Divisions began into those better and worse. Brother was an enemy of brother, and brother killed brother. Man dominated woman, his companion, and made her obedient to himself. He humiliated the one who gives life. Man turned clear rivers, crystalline lakes, seas and oceans into foul-smelling sewage. He cut down forests and killed animals. And he turned air into poisonous gas. He proclaimed moolah his new god.

And Gaia wept. "They are killing me. I am dying" she said to the Creator.

And God looked at his Paradise and wept too. And then God stopped the world. And he said, "Remember what I said when I offered you this gift. I said: Love one another, respect each other, live in harmony, health, procreate and be happy. Everything you need you have received from me for free. Love, health, happiness and life in Paradise, which is this beautiful planet. Why did you choose Darkness and Fear? Why did you choose wars, quarrels, divisions and hatred? Why do you throw stones at your brothers? Why don't you respect yourselves? Why can't you love? Why do you reject love and light? You've already done it once. Then I stopped the world with water. So that you would also stop. But you have not understood the Father's lesson. Now I stopped the world with air. So that you would also stop. Will you understand this time? Next time, I will stop the world with fire.

March 2020

The World Stopped

Rainbow

$\mathbf{F}$our, dressed in black, riders stood on a high mountain and looked at the world, as if admiring their work. Masses of dark, heavy clouds were swirling over their heads. Darkness reigned all around. Like four winds, the riders came silently from the four corners of the world, leaving behind clouds of dark dust. Faces covered with black masks, and in empty eyes without expression, it would be difficult to find any feelings. Each hand was dressed in a leather glove. Long black capes hung from the shoulders, which waved like bat wings while riding. They looked like four terrible beasts.

"It went easily," said the rider on the white horse in a hollow, as if soundless voice.

"Yes," the rider on the red horse confirmed, and his voice was even more colorless. "They always react the same."

"An illusion was enough," added the third rider on a black horse.

"Yes," said the fourth rider riding a dead-pale horse, as if reflecting. – The illusion of an invisible war with an invisible enemy for invisible goods. People hungry for what they can't find in themselves. Fear and Pride have always been my greatest allies."

Suddenly, a strong gust of wind swept above their heads. The four capes began to flutter, making the beasts look even scarier. The horses moved, shuffling their hooves, as if feeling that something was coming. The wind began to chase away the dark clouds. Suddenly, the earth was illuminated by a blinding ray of sun. The riders looked up, and when they looked back, there was a fifth rider standing in front of them. His outfit was white and his horse with a long mane was also white. Head and face uncovered. Shoulder-length hair moved gently in the now light wind.

And so, they stood opposite each other—Darkness and Light. United Forces of Darkness against the only force of Light. Pestilence, War, Famine and Death opposite Love.

"You have raised your hand again against my people," said the rider in white with power in his voice, albeit calmly.

"We only do what we are called to do. " The fourth rider on the pale horse replied.

"I'm not the one killing. It's Fear and Pride. I'm just reaping my toll."

"Little faith, much Fear in your people," said the black rider on the white horse. "We gave them only what they want and what they are chasing. We gave them the Illusion," added the rider on the black horse.

"We have fed their Pride. This time the War brought them together, though it separated them, and Fear united," said the rider on the red horse.

"You underestimate my people. The unawakened are already waking up. And one awakened awakens a

hundred others. You have taken only those who have chosen the Illusion and do not want to wake up."

Saying that, the white rider looked to the right. The black riders followed his gaze. And behold, they saw an endless crowd of people heading towards them, with calmness and a smile on their faces. Women, men, young, old, children. And each of them held a small torch in his hand, like a lit match.

The crowd stopped on the right of the white rider.

"Are you not afraid of Disease?" The black rider on the white horse asked.

"Try to approach me," a young woman hugging a baby in her arms said in a calm voice. The black rider spurred his horse trying to ride up to her, but his horse only spun in circles as if unable to move forward. As if there was an invisible wall between him and the woman.

"Evil will not come to me if I do not open the door to it," said a young man standing next to the woman. "Are you not afraid of War?" asked the rider on the red horse.

"Goodness does not fight. It doesn't have to. Goodness wins with Goodness. If Goodness began to fight, it would no longer be Good. Goodness itself is victory," said an elderly man from the crowd.

"Are you not afraid of Famine?" The black horse rider asked.

"You can't take something from me that's not in me. And everything I need I have in me. And I get everything I ask for," answered a middle-aged woman with a gentle smile.

"Are you not afraid of Death?" The fourth rider on the dead-pale horse asked at the end.

"And why should I be afraid of you?" asked a man of mature age." I died many times before I learned to live and understood that you are only an Illusion. All of us who are walking here have died to be born again and to live. Death is an Illusion.

The four black horse riders bowed their heads, as knights who lost in battle do. After a while, however, the fourth rider once again looked at the people and asked.

"Where is your strength from?"

Then an elderly old woman stepped out in front of the crowd and looking the Beast straight into the eyes, said calmly and quietly, although in her voice Power was enormous:

'Love conquers everything." Then, pointing with her hand at the white rider, she said, "He has conquered the world. He is the way, the truth and the life. We trusted Him, and He taught us how to live. He showed that Love is the Way, and the heart is the Signpost. And where there is Love, there is no Fear, War, Hunger and Disease. He who grabs the sword perishes by the sword. I don't have an iron sword like you do, and yet you are the one who is afraid to approach me. My shield is Love. My strength is Love. It is all of us," she pointed to the crowd behind her, "who are the salt of the earth and the light of light. We are One."

The fourth rider lowered his head, defeated.

Without moving, the White Rider looked into the eyes of each of the four black ones and said four times, "I love you. I am setting you free." And when he barely finished saying it, the Wind of Renewal flew in. And he carried away the Beasts of Darkness, lifting them in the form of red clouds, upwards, to the Source. The black knights threw off their masks. And behold, they appeared on horseback, in the form of beautiful white Angels. And each of them carried a different message. The Plague became Health, War became Peace, Hunger became Abundance, and Death became Life.

"Done!" said Love.

In the blue sky a huge colorful rainbow appeared which entwined the whole world.

April 2020

You Are Not Alone

The woman was sitting on a bench that was part of the coastal amphitheater by the beach. Her gaze was fixed on the dark, calm surface of the ocean, merging with the starry sky. The sun has already set some time ago. The space around her was deserted. The people who come in large numbers every day to this place to watch the wonderful, full of amazing and difficult to describe in earthly words, colors of the sunset over the Pacific, have left. Only somewhere nearby there was one man sitting. He looked like he had fallen asleep. Actually, she should be leaving too, but this silence interspersed with the sound of the ocean waves, this peace and this magic of the place, made her want to stop this moment.

She looked longingly at the stars and, as if habitually, began to look for this one, the only one...hers. She's been doing this for as long as she can remember. She was looking for her home, somewhere high up in the stars. She kept her eyes on the diamonds of the sky winking at her alluringly, and she still felt lost. Lost in the Cosmos and lost in that earthly quasi-reality whose unreality she saw and felt so clearly. A reality that was just a screened film. Hologram. But people called it cinema and this earthly theatre a reality. They seemed as if hypnotized. They called the Dream the Reality and the Reality the Dream. They called their false Ego logic, and their wise and very logical soul, Illusion. As if they had made a mistake. It's like they've forgotten who they are. Instead of love, they chose conflicts and wars. Instead of health – everything that did not serve this health. Instead of Truth, they chose Lies, which they called their Truths. Instead of being free, they preferred to be afraid. They were stuck in fear and earthly divisions, calling it freedom. They themselves voluntarily became slaves of matter. They put on thousands of masks. They were silent when they should be talking, and they shouted when they should be silent. They chose matter instead of happiness and love. They dreamed their dream of sheep in a corral and did not want to wake up from this dream. They respected neither their planet nor the time they were given to stay on it.

This feeling of loss, loneliness and some kind of indefinite longing has accompanied her since she was a child. For some reason, which she herself did not understand, she thought and talked about herself as girl from the stars. She was still looking for answers to the questions "Who am I? And why am I here?" She felt like someone had thrown her into this Earthly Matrix and left her alone. As if she didn't fit into this man-made world. Although, in fact, it was through those whom man called gods and to whom he gave power over himself, that he worshipped and chose fear.

There was still a kind of surprise that so many people talking about love didn't really understand that love at all. And with the word "love" on their lips, they decided about guilt and punishment and who was better and who was worse. Who deserves forgiveness and who doesn't. And invoking the so-called Logic, they confused everything that was simple. They did not see the simplest solutions. And the simplest of all solutions was exactly Love.

Now she was looking at the stars again and again she felt that somewhere out there, on one of the distant Pleiades, was her real home and family. A house of love. Again, she felt that piercing painful longing. And unexpectedly for herself, she said out loud:

"Where are you, my brothers and sisters?" Why did you leave me here?

And suddenly something unexpected happened. Suddenly, she saw figures coming down from the mountain, as if flowing, bright, smiling. They looked like five angels. She recognized them immediately. "You came," she said loudly, and tears of emotion appeared in her eyes. She felt relief, joy and a wave of soothing, warm, peaceful absolute love enveloping her body, as if from the inside.

"We've always been here. With you. You've never been alone," she heard, but it was not an earthly voice. It was a voice in her head.

The luminous, ethereal figures approached her and if surrounded her with the warmth of their energy. She felt as if, after a long journey, she had finally returned home to her most beloved family. Finally, she felt safe. She felt calm. She looked lovingly at their faces, on which there was joy and that elfin expression of amusement. She knew them all, though she still didn't know where they came from. She still couldn't remember their names.

"I knew, I felt you were somewhere nearby, but I didn't see you. Why?" She asked in her mind, as if not noticing that she had switched to telepathic conversation mode. As if this way of communication was something completely natural for her.

"Because you didn't trust yourself. Because you empathized with your earthly role so much that you forgot who you are and why you came here."

"And who am I? Where is my home?"

"Your hone is in the Pleiades. You are our sister."

"Why am I here?"

"To lead people to the other side of the bridge."

"You're talking about dimensions. I have to teach them love to grow and remind them of who they are. Is that right?"

"Isn't it you who people call the earthly angel telling fairy tales? Fairy tales are our specialty. We are cosmic storytellers."

"Some people actually say that" she smiled. "But people believe in different things. Even in angels."

"Because that's how they were taught. Because that's what they want. People need to believe in something, and they need authorities."

"I know. It is sad how lost humanity has become. People need guides.'

"And you are one. That's what you came here for. You have come down from a higher dimension to lead them. Remind yourself. You have never had authorities. You were one for yourself. You were only looking for knowledge, not opinions."

"That's true...And do I also have a guide?"

"You are the guide. Also, ours, but also yours. You are our older sister. When you undertook this task on earth, you asked us for help. You have written a very detailed scenario in which you have included all possible variants of earthly choices. You have prepared yourself at length and very meticulously for this mission and for this role. You forbade us to show ourselves until the time came. But we were always there. And sometimes we were sad when we saw you get lost in the labyrinth of earthly life. And sometimes you made us laugh to tears when you didn't see what you were looking at. It's like you were playing hide-and-seek with yourself. Earthly life is the greatest theatre for the viewer, but also for the actor. Especially when this play 'My Life' that people perform here is as interesting as your life. You proceeded through these earthly storms with your head held high and bravely faced them."

The faces of those who came from the stars were still in smiles and their joy was also inside her. She had the impression that they had a lot of fun with her earthly amnesia. Everything she had just heard began to fall into place. Her whole life.

Although, in fact, she always knew it somewhere inside. "And the others?" She asked.

"The majority of people need guides. Some guides operate on the spiritual platform, and others in a similar way as you. However, such a mission is always associated with rejection. People are often deaf to the voice of their spiritual guides. They doubt whether this is true and reject it. That is why earthly guides are needed. Guides speaking in an earthly voice. However, the Darkness defends its power over the world of the Matrix and throws stones at those who expose its face. Only the bravest of us choose to be earthly guides of Light. Guides are like teachers, and their students themselves become guides and teachers. And so, man leads man across the bridge between dimensions. Man teaches man to fly."

"And this is the time of transition...," she said in reverie.

"Yes. This is the time of transition. A certain stage in the history of the world is just ending. It's as if an experiment is ending. And this is the moment of decision. That is why so many people wake up in this Darkness and look for their way home. People either choose Light, in other words Freedom and Love, that is return home, or they will remain in the Darkness of their fear corral. And Darkness knows it. That's why it attacks so hard."

"Where am I going?"

"Where you have to go."

"Why am I not afraid of the Dark?

"Because Darkness has no power over you. You are the light. It is Darkness that fears you. That's why it screams so much. That is why it throws so many stones. That's what fear is. Fear screams because it is afraid. Fear divides because it is afraid. Fear fights because it is afraid. Fear controls because it is afraid. Love does not fight. If Love fought, it would not be Love, but War or the Angel of Darkness. Love conquers with love."

In that instance the woman noticed that the man sitting nearby on the bench moved, as if awakened from a dream. He got up and spun around, as if he were looking around. It was an older man. His face was confused. The man approached her and, in a slightly uncertain voice, said:

"I'm sorry that I'm bothering you. I fell asleep and just woke up. But I don't see well, and I think I'm lost. I don't know where I am. It's dark and I don't know the way. It was only a few days ago that I moved to this area. I forgot my phone where I had navigation. I can't call anyone to ask because I can't remember the numbers. Could you help me find my way home?"

"Of course," the woman smiled. "Together we will try to find your way and your home. Please take my hand. You are no longer alone."
Behind the man's back, she saw joyful and smiling luminous figures which were disappearing into their dimension. And although she did not see them with earthly eyes, she saw them with the eyes of the soul. She was already sure that she was not alone. And she never was.

Guardian Of Time

A woman sat in the park on a bench right next to the water. She liked to come here, and she liked her silence. Although this silence was not silence at all, although it was. The rustling of the wind dancing in the leaves of the trees, the sound of water flowing into the pond, the singing of birds, the splash of a jumping fish, quacking ducks, gaggling wild geese, and somewhere in the distance the joyful screams of children playing and the sound of conversations of people walking. Someone rode a bicycle, a dog barked somewhere. A plane flew upstairs. And yet silence. As if time had stopped. But it was flowing.

The woman watched all this as if locked in some kind of space-time bubble, in which there is neither time nor space. She was here and now, and at the same time she was in another world. In a world of her own thoughts and her imagination. As if she were in two worlds at the same time.

She was thinking about her life so far. About how everything was perfectly arranged in it. It could seem as if it had been planned in advance, before she was even born. A detailed script, somewhere up there, in another dimension. And every element of her life, like a puzzle, perfectly combined with other seemingly distant events. She thought about the consequences of every decision made or not made at some point, and how every person she met in life was for something. And also, about how everything in her life had its time. As if someone was watching over it, so that everything happened exactly when it was supposed to happen.

She thought about what she hadn't done. About her missed opportunities. She recalled a friend from her early youth. They were teenagers at the time. The friend played tennis very well, she played table tennis. He offered to teach her his game. It ended up with one or two visits to the court. She didn't do well, so she gave up. And then she thought about it all her life. About the fact that she would have liked to be able to play tennis. And the thought was coming back– You gave up quickly, girl. One failure was enough, and you decided it wasn't for you. You doubted yourself. You didn't trust yourself. You didn't take advantage of that time. And somehow, she never had the opportunity to go back to it and learn how to play tennis. Although perhaps there were opportunities, but somehow there was no more time for it. Something else was important.

And as she thought about these various missed opportunities, how everything has its time in this life and how perfectly arranged it is, suddenly an older, tall, slim man in a hat stood in front of her. He appeared as if out of nowhere.

Or maybe she just didn't notice him, immersed in her thoughts and in her world. She looked at him with a surprised and somewhat unconscious look, as if someone or something had violently thrown her into earthly reality. The man was serious, his face stern, his eyes piercing. He exuded calm and strength. But it was not an earthly force. This force flowed from within. And there was something strangely familiar in him, though she couldn't say what it was. As if she had known him forever. She felt friendship, but also respect at the same time. He smiled at her gently, but as if invisibly. He looked at the spot next to her, as if without words he was asking if he could sit there. The woman also answered without words–yes. The conversation began strangely.

They sat in silence for a moment. But she didn't feel abashed. She had the impression that she is sitting next to a friend with whom she could simply remain silent. She returned to her thoughts about the passage of time and its perfect script.

"Time is your life," she suddenly heard the silent, deep, but pleasant voice of the stranger she knew. Did he read her thoughts?

"It's beautiful here," she replied, as if not wanting to admit to her thoughts.

"Life on earth is beautiful, only some do not notice it. They forgot."

"How did they forget it?" She asked surprised.

"They just forgot. Just as they forgot why they came here into this life. It's time for them to remind themselves."

"I don't understand. How are they supposed to remind themselves?

"Time has stopped so that they will remind themselves. Time has accelerated and slowed down at the same time."

"How can time speed up and slow down at the same time?" The woman was more and more intrigued.

"Time can do anything."

"What does it mean that time has accelerated and slowed down at the same time?

"Time gave people time to understand what they were supposed to understand. However, people did not want to understand. And the time given for this lesson is just ending. Therefore, time accelerated, accelerating events and stopped at the same time. It kept people in their lives to remind them what they had forgotten."

"And what are people supposed to understand?"

"What is really important in life. And who they are and why they came here into this life."

"And what is important in life?"

"You don't have to ask about it. You've always known that intuitively. That's why you never got attached to matter. You have been and are free. There is no fear in you."

The woman did not answer. She pondered the old man's response. Like in a kaleidoscope, various situations from her life flashed through her head. "Yes...he is right..." she thought. She easily closed the door of the past and went into the new, though unknown, with confidence and some kind of faith that she would manage, and everything would be fine. And it was. Different, but always interesting. Like on a trip. Although she also happened to stop once, somewhere for a longer time and not listen to the inner voice. That was the time when she was suffering.   A time when she wanted to stop time. Unsuccessfully.

"Man cannot stop time." Said the man as if in response to her thoughts.

"And who controls time?"

"Guardians of time.

"Guardians of time?" Her curiosity grew with each passing moment. "Who are the guardians of time?"

"The guards make sure that everything happens at the right time. They can shorten or lengthen the time, they can speed it up, slow it down or stop it."

"And can they repeat the time?"

"No time is the same twice, just as there isn't the same water twice flowing in the river. Time flows like a river. And everything is assigned to a given time. A moment in history."

"Does this mean that everything is written in advance?"

"Everything leads where it is supposed to lead. Everything has its place in time, and everything is for something. Although some believe that everything is a series of coincidences. Human naivety and unbelief." He sighed almost inaudibly at the last sentence.

"Every event you experience and every person you meet have their place, time and meaning. Every leader or politician is also appointed for a given time and is for something. People are just passers-by in your life, just like you are a passer-by in their life. You are simply given time together at a certain time. Sometimes longer, sometimes shorter, but it is always the time you give to each other. And it is you who decide on the quality of this time."

The woman became pensive again. She remembered how she had once given someone a watch, and many years later someone had gifted her with a watch. She began to wonder if these situations were somehow connected with each other. Again, the older man, as if reading her thoughts, replied. This time it didn't surprise her anymore.

"Your time was up then, but you didn't want to go any further. You stuck to the old and wanted to stop time. And then the guard had to intervene. He was the one who gave you the thought, appeared as a watchmaker and sold you a beautiful watch, which you then lovingly gave to that man. A beautiful and expensive watch, because it was a beautiful and precious time in your life. In this way, the guard offered you his time and shortened your time with that man. Because each of you had to go your own way. Then time sped up. A lot was happening in a short time. But you suffered because you didn't leave at the right time. And when you overcame the suffering, time slowed down, and you started smiling again."

"You said that the guards make sure that everything takes place at the right time. So why didn't I leave sooner?"

"Man has free will and does not always listen to the voice of his soul. He often clings to the old time. And each time has its own guardian. When time changes, the old guardian of time leaves and the new one comes with a new time. And when a person does not want to enter into the new and understand what is supposed to be understood, then the guard accelerates time and events. It is often associated with pain and upheaval in life or history."

"And what happened when, many years later, someone else gave me a watch?"

"History has come full circle. It was repeated, although vice versa and at a different time."

"I don't understand."

"Then you also suffered after parting with someone you loved and who loved you. But this time you didn't try to stop time. You trusted yourself and left. Subconsciously, you knew that this was not your time yet. You both had to understand something else and experience something separately. Go other ways to reach the intersection where your paths have crossed again. You told the man that you would meet in five years and talk. You have determined the time.   Then another watchmaker appeared in your life, who led you through the difficult time of transition for you after parting. At the end, he gave you a watch. He cut your time off from a man in half. The watchmaker gave you his own time. And now he could leave and make room for a new time and a new guard."

"And why did I meet this man when we weren't ready for this love? Doesn't that mean it wasn't our time?"

But it was your time. If you had not experienced the happiness of that love and then the pain of separation, you would not have understood what your love is and how important it is. You would not be able to value this love."

"All of this is strange. But it makes sense. And while it's hard to understand, it seems so simple when you talk about it." The woman thought again and remembered the second watchmaker.

"You know," she said, "when I went through that difficult time after the second breakup, I couldn't decide for a long-time which way to take in my new life. Apparently, I had many roads ahead of me and each one seemed interesting, but I was drawn only to one road. However, for some reason, I was still hesitant. And then I met that watchmaker again. Apparently, he was healthy, as if everything was fine, and yet I had the impression that life escapes from him. As if he was fading before my eyes. And then I thought that I no longer had time to think about choosing the path and postpone life until tomorrow. I trusted myself and set out on the path I had chosen in the beginning. And something strange happened.

The other roads, as if intertwined with the most important one..." The woman thought again for a moment, then in reverie she said "And then the watchmaker left..." Again, she became pensive and after a while continued her story. "And when I entered this new road, everything went quickly. Everything was favorable for me. All the doors opened. New people appeared with their hand outstretched to help. It was as if I was surrounded by earthly angels who were just waiting to help me and carry me on their wings through all the meanders of the river so that I could soar high. As if a new time and a new energy."

"That's how the guards leave. Quietly and noiselessly. And so come the new guards with a new time. They come with panache." Said a stranger thoughtfully.

Again, they sat for a moment without saying anything. The woman watched the ducks walking with wobbling steps, approaching people without fear. They just walked where they wanted. As if they knew that this space around the water belongs to them.

"And what about loved ones who die?" She asked suddenly.

"They don't die. They just go home. Their time is up. They came here to give someone their time and bring that person to a predetermined harbor. And then they leave so that this person can live."

"What is time?"

"Time is like playing tennis. It requires fitness, reflexes, watch-making precision and intuition. When you catch the ball, it's like catching your moment at a given time. Exactly at this given moment. If you do not react properly, you are late, the ball will fly away. Moment in time will fly away irretrievably. You start a new game because you can't go back to the old one or repeat it. However, you can win this new game if you learn to play and catch the ball. Catch your moments. Because time, like life, consists of moments. From used or missed opportunities. And at the end of this game, you remember all those passed balls and all those missed chances. That is why it is worth catching your moments. Fitness in life is also useful," he added with a slight, barely visible smile. "Fitness is your health. It is worth taking care of yourself."

"And thus, the end became the beginning." This time the woman smiled, recalling her thoughts from the beginning of this strange conversation.

"It's time for me," said the familiar stranger as he got up from the bench. "It's time for the new." Saying this, he bowed slightly as if to say, "Thank you for this time together."

The woman watched the man walking away. She had the impression as if life was escaping him. As if he was fading before her eyes.

"Thank you for this time together, guard." She said quietly, smiling lightly and as if gratefully.

"Thank you for coming to say goodbye to me. It was a good time, and it is just over. It's time to go into the new. How the new will be is only up to me. This time, I'll catch all the balls. It will be a very good round. Very good time. The best."

July 2020

Bench In the Park

A bench. It stands alone in the park. Right on the water's edge. And the view from it is beautiful. Sometimes someone will sit down for a short time, ponder and maybe for the first time in life will see another world. The world of the soul. He had seen this world before, but without reflection, without noticing. There were only words. Empty words.

The magical bench that gives peace and rest. Soothing of all the senses. Emotions. It allows you to organize your thoughts or not think at all. To be here and now. Enjoy the silence. Immerse yourself in silence. To give respite to the weary of hustle and bustle of the human world, to the ears. It allows the eyes to see more.

This bench is like stopping in time. Stopping in life. In its rush to...exactly...often you don't even know what. But you rush, rush, and rush. You rush blindly doing a lot of unnecessary things that you consider the credo of your life. You judge, criticize, decry. You run without stopping after the matter from which you have made your god. You prostrate before matter and worship it. For matter you are able to do a lot, and even more. Is this what your life is about? About the pursuit of matter? That's why you came into this life, to accumulate treasures of matter on earth?

Time runs through fingers like water. The time's clock measures its time backwards. Measures days and hours. And there are fewer and fewer of them. How much time do you have left? Maybe an hour? Maybe a day, a week, a year? Maybe a few years. You don't know. You naively believe that you are immortal, even though you have only one life to live. And this time is limited. And this life is just a few moments on this earth. Because death is everyone's destiny. And there is no escaping it. So, when do you want to start living? When do you want to reach for your dreams? When do you want to be happy? Or is this the time to do it now? At this point. Now. And not to postpone life until tomorrow. For later.

A lonely bench in the park. It would seem that it is waiting for someone. Maybe for you? It invites you to sit down and just be in that one moment. To stop. To last. To appreciate that one moment. To encounter oneself. So that you feel a gentle gust of air on your face. A kiss of the wind. Hear the quiet melody of nature. The murmur of water. The sound of dancing leaves in the branches of trees. To listen to the conversation of geese and ducks walking along the shore, who live together and next to each other in unison. They coexist in peace. This magical bench in the park invites you and wants to show you the beauty of the sun reflected in the water. A different world. It encourages you to look up at the sky and notice the images and signs depicted in the shape of white clouds. To touch the grass with your bare foot and to feel one with mother earth. To feel that you are part of this nature. To understand that the Earth is your home. Our joint home. And we all are one race, one family. Brother and sister.

"Earthlings, children, how do you take care of your home?" Someone asks high above. "How do you manage the planet that I have given you to be in charge of? How do you take care of each other? What do you do to brother and sister? Why do you condemn your brothers and sisters to hunger, homelessness and suffering? Why do you throw stones at each other? What do you do to yourselves and why do you choose fear and war over love? How do you use the gift of life that I have given you?

And when you understand all this, peace and joy come. And there is only love. And where there is love, the impossible becomes possible."

And here a woman sits down on the bench. And although time has measured many Earth years in her earthly calendar, she seems to be younger than when she was younger. A magnetizing aura is emanating from her, a bright light. She went through a lot in her life and walked many roads. She looked into hell to choose heaven. To choose love and choose herself. To win her life. And now there is peace and acceptance on her face. The eyes look at the world with the wisdom of experience.

The bench welcomes the guest with gratitude and offers the best of its best. Peace, quiet and joy of experiencing the moment. That moment. Wild, though tame birds come closer, as if attracted by an invisible thread of divine energy. As if they felt the significance of this moment. And this moment is important. Because this is the moment. The wind embraces the branches of the trees and dances a joyful dance with them. The sun comes out from behind the clouds and illuminates the world with the glow of warm light. The earth rejoices, and with it the whole Universe rejoices.

A man approaches the bench. He is determined. He already knows. He has already chosen. He is already sure. He grew up to love and opened his heart to love. He understood that it is not matter, not struggle and flight from love, but love that is the way, the truth and the goal of life. And that understanding brought him to this very park and to this bench. For a heart filled with love will always find its way to another heart filled with love. And even if these two hearts are separated by eons of light, they will always attract each other to unite in love and create One.

The man sits down next to the woman. His eyes look into her eyes and merge together in the endless ocean of another dimension. And when the eyes speak, then the words become superfluous. The woman smiles at the man. He silently takes her hand, as if saying,

"You are here. It took a while, but I finally found you. Because I found myself. Dance with me, girl. May this moment together last forever. Let me hold your hand and walk beside you and with you on the same path. Together."

The woman reciprocates his hand's touch and puts her head on the man's shoulder. And it's good. So good. And there is no longer a lonely bench in the park. And sitting on the same bench, snuggled up to each other, the woman and the man with a smile look at the world with the same eyes. Two roads merge into one. Two houses become one. Divisions disappear. Wars are fading into oblivion. Female energy and masculine energy combine as equal partners. Cooperate. Two becomes One. Mother Gaia smiles and the Father in heaven rejoices. Let this moment last.

Plant

It happened once that on the road right next to the house where I live, I saw a small Plant in a pot. It would seem that this Plant fell from the sky.

It was an ordinary black plastic pot. Ordinary. Ugly. But the Plant was pretty, although somehow inconspicuous. As if she was missing something. As if something had been taken from her. As if she couldn't breathe. She reminded me of a beautiful girl who had been dressed in a gray Cinderella dress, with tight, uncomfortable shoes on her feet which made her forget who she really was. A girl who has lost her natural joy. A girl whose freedom has been taken away. The breath of life. A girl who believed she was inferior.

The pot stood in a shady place on the flowerbed among other planted in soil plants, which benefited from the abundance of benefits of Mother Earth and lushly climbed upwards, showing all their beauty. And this small, inconspicuous Plant was still locked in this too tight, black, ugly pot without soil. No oxygen. No food. No love. Like in a prison. Almost invisible.

I looked and thought, "Probably someone left her here absent-mindedly. Forgot. But he will be looking. Maybe a gardener. He will return. He will come here for her." I passed, went my own way and forgot.

The next day, the situation repeated itself. I looked, made a note in my head, and walked away. But on the third day, when I saw her again, I stopped. The pot with the Plant stood in exactly the same place. As if she was waiting for me. And indeed. I looked at her attentively and she spoke. I heard a quiet:

"I'm waiting for you here. Take care of me."

"Come with me. I'll remind you who you are." I replied.

I took the plant in my hand and carried her home. A note was glued to the ugly pot with the inscription: Hibiscus. I smiled. What symbolism. As if someone up there was suggesting something and showing the way. As if he were saying, "Here's the answer you're looking for."

I took the Plant home. I took her out of the ugly black pot, in which instead of life-giving soil there was only an artificial imitation of some substance that was only supposed to pretend to be soil. It was an illusion of something that someone was supposed to believe was something other than what it was. And it was just ordinary garbage. A lie.

With great care I transplanted her into a larger pot. For some reason, I chose a white one. I put her in a sunny place so that it had access to light and watered her regularly. I took care of her. And everything I did for her, I did with love. I was feeding her with love. She was very close to me. I liked to look at her. I watched her make friends with neighboring plants, how she grew, and how she sprouted new leaves and shoots. At first it was as if quietly, as if a little uncertain, as if looking around. However, every day more and more courageously. With more trust, confidence and self-confidence. She looked like she was learning a new life she hadn't known before. She was learning herself. Like the Little Mermaid who, having dropped her fish tail, learned to move in the New World. And each step, painful at first, became much more lighter. Effortless. Until it became a beautiful dance. And the Plant seemed to savor more and more her freedom and the new strength she was discovering in herself every day. She was getting more and more beautiful. She was bubbling with more energy. Wonderful energy of life. Nourished by love, she found love in herself and became love herself.

A few days, maybe weeks, maybe months, had passed. And here, I found myself in a shopping mall. I found myself in the main square in the city. Suddenly, in the midst of a gray, masked crowd of faceless people, I saw a beautiful girl dressed in white. Her outfit was simple, but at the same time elegant. Not a designer outfit. My attention was drawn to well done, comfortable, tasteful shoes. Shoes a traveler in space-time needs, who went on a long journey and with curiosity travels through new lands. A light, small, leather backpack hung over the girl's right shoulder, matching the color of the ankle boots. It contained only what could serve on this journey. No unnecessary things. No unnecessary baggage.

She walked courageously, without a mask, genuine in her truth. Strong with her inner strength. On her face there were simultaneously peace and joy. Love in her eyes. She smiled at everyone. She looked like an angel who had descended from heaven to this planet.

She stood out from the crowd so much that she caught the attention of everyone around her. Eyes from behind masked faces followed her. They watched with curiosity, admiration and a kind of longing. It was as if they saw something they had lost somewhere in themselves and could not find the key to the vault. And this was the key to the Truth about oneself. About who I really am. The key that opens the prison of fear. Because where there is fear, there is confusion and there are masks. Where there is fear, there is no love. There is only fear and there are masks. Costumes. Actors acting in the earthly theater of life. Truth is freedom. And Truth is absolute love. The girl exuded energy magnetizing others. She was the Truth in itself. Pure Truth. She was Love.

Men approached her spontaneously. As if attracted by an invisible force that they could not resist. The power of feminine energy. By the power of Truth. The power of Love that this girl was. They asked if they could say hello. They complimented her. They gave gifts. They asked what they could do for her. They were mesmerized by her beauty. They couldn't take their eyes off her. And she was just smiling. And in her left hand she held a beautiful orange flower that seemed to be an out-of-this-world plant. A plant from the sky.

I knew this girl. She once told me her story. There was a lot of pain, rejection, misunderstanding. But there was also great strength and courage in telling the truth, choosing your own paths. However, the world of Fear does not like Otherness. The World of Fear is afraid of Otherness. The World of Fear is afraid of the Truth. The World of Fear rejects Otherness and stones the individual.

And it happened that traveling the world of darkness of fear, the girl from the stars lost her way. She went to the hell of depression. Her beautiful, joyful smile was obscured by the shadow of sadness. The shoes became uncomfortable, the clothes gray and torn, and the backpack heavy with stones. And the Girl forgot who she was and why she was here. She forgot where her home was. Although somewhere inside she felt and as if she knew that her home was not from this world of darkness. She looked up at the sky full of stars and asked, crying: "Who am I?" Where is my home?" She looked at the stars and complained like a child: "It's so dark here. So cold. So dense. It's so hard to breathe. It's so hard to fly."

I met her by the ocean. She stared in silence at the dancing waves and their melodious noise. I saw her light, covered with a gray robe, and I saw her sadness. She was so fragile and so strong at the same time. She had within her the great power of the divine warrior of light. But she forgot about it.

I sat down next to her and hugged her. She clung to me like a frightened, love-hungry child.

"Do not be afraid," I said, stroking her beautiful hair "You don't have to be afraid of anything anymore. You are not alone. You never were. I'm here."

"I'm lost." She whispered through tears. "I don't know where my home is. I don't know who I am. Can you help me? Can you show the way? How to get out of this hell? How to get out of this prison?"

"There is only one way. The way up. This is the path to freedom."

„Will you help me?"

"Yes. I will help you recall who you are. I will help you find what you have lost."

"Where is the key to open the gates of this prison of hell?"

"You have this key. That key is in you. And that key is love. Love yourself. When you do that, you'll remember who you are. Love is the key to the gates of heaven. Love is Freedom. Fear is a prison."

"How do I do it? How do I love myself?"

"Take care of your Plant in yourself. Become a conscious gardener."

And now I saw this beautiful girl again. I saw an angel who had once lost the path in a dark world ruled by fear and had forgotten who she was. But sometimes you have to get lost to find yourself. Paradoxically, hell can be an awakening of consciousness. Understanding. Death and resurrection.

Finding the way home. The road to the source. Road to oneself. And this beautiful girl who once believed she was Cinderella did just that. She found Love in herself. She learned to love herself. She nurtured this love until she herself became Love. And this love gave her the angelic Power. From an inconspicuous plant, the girl became a beautiful heavenly flower.

The next day, I looked up at the morning sky. It was dawning. And in the midst of gray, heavy, sad clouds, I saw beautiful orange hues of light. And that light was so beautiful that I couldn't take my eyes off it. It looked like a host of angels surrounding this planet with their angelic protection. Suddenly, I felt great, great joy. A spontaneous smile appeared on my face. I had the impression that a new, gentle energy was flowing down to the ground. Like a girl, I swirled around. And suddenly my eyes fell on the Plant. And then I saw it. A beautiful orange flower that bloomed thanks to love. Thus, the Plant repaid for the effort put into her care.

"The night is behind us." I thought. "A new Day is rising. What this New Day will be like depends only on me. Because I create this Day. So let it be the Day of Love and Joy.

January 2022

Turtle

I saw Him from afar. On the way to the parking lot. I got out of the way. I sat quietly on the grass and watched him for a while. He used to run away. This time he stayed. As if the fear had passed.

At some point, I realized that I had stopped motionless like Him. I stopped in life. I stopped on the way to the parking lot. Between the bench, trees and water. Away from the world. There was only Nature, He and I. Time stopped and I stopped. Zero thoughts, no unnecessary emotions. Total silence inside. Serenity. Harmony. Unity. And I thought, "It's good. So good. This is our moment."

And He seemed to hear my thoughts. At one point, slowly, without haste, at his tortoise pace, he stretched his neck even more, turned his head towards me and, seemingly without looking, began to observe me. First, just with one eye. Apparently casually. The other eye was looking at the water. I looked too.

And I saw a Mirror. And emotions in this Mirror. And this Mirror was as if divided in half. Part of the mirror, on the other side of the lake, as if far from us, was wrinkled by a gust of wind. It seemed to flow. As if the water was chasing itself. The wave chased the wave. Emotion chased emotion. The second part of the Mirror, the one on our side, was perfectly smooth. Silence. Serenity. Balance.

And in this whole mirror were reflected trees, sky, clouds, sun, birds. The entire world. However, the image on our side seemed to be clear and harmonious compared to the crooked image reflected in the emotionally wrinkled water, somewhere far away from us. As if in another world, although in the same one.

And suddenly, as if awakened from reflections, I heard that I thought, "This water is uneven. On one side the surface seems to have a bulge." I smiled to myself as if I answered myself. "That's what Illusion is. The illusion of life. A crooked mirror."

I looked at Him again. As if I wanted to tell him this. But it turned out that it was He who looked at me with a playful twinkle in his eye. And as if he were saying, "I already know that." Then he blinked and slowly, without haste, at his tortoise pace turned his head towards the water. Again he froze motionless, and I with him.

And again we were looking in the same direction. Towards the sun. We observed the same thing. We were next to each other, but as if connected by an invisible thread of light energy. Time seemed to have stopped again. "It's good. So good." A white bird sang. "This is our moment." The second bird sang. The wind carried these words further. "It's good. So good." The water hummed. "Good..." The tree branches rustled. Two white birds performed a love dance in the air.

After a while, though it is difficult to say how long it took, He turned his head again. He looked at me as if confused and ashamed. As if awakened from a deep sleep. Shy in his shyness, but confident in his confidence in what he is doing. As if with an apology and an invitation at the same time. As if he were saying,

"I'm sorry it took so long. I'm sorry I slept so long. Sorry I didn't listen. I'm sorry I ran away. I don't want to look at you from afar anymore. Shake my hand, girl. Stand next to me. Stand by me. Let's dance together. The road is wide and beautiful ahead of us. Bright. We will walk this path together holding hands. Looking in the same direction. We are not afraid of storms, because the storms stayed far behind us. In another world. There is only the Wisdom of experience and the Love of the heart. You are. I am. We are. A One. I already know. I understood."

Two white birds made another full circle above our heads. "It's good. So good." The bird sang. "This is our moment." The second bird sang. The wind carried these words further. "It's good. So good." The water hummed. "Good..." The tree branches rustled. And again time stopped, but as if it was flowing at its own pace. As if in another dimension. As if time wanted to give us time. But a different time. Time without storms. A time of sun and joy. A time of love.

"This is our moment," He said. "I already know that. I already understand. And I'll never let you go again.

This moment is eternity. This moment is Unity. This moment is Harmony. This moment is our life."

May 2022

Flower

When everything around looks the same, attention is attracted by what is different. Otherness attracts otherness. With its beauty. Color. Courage. Freedom. Intrigues. Makes curious. Otherness teaches. Otherness shows the way. It evokes emotions. Otherness says,

"Stop. Look in my direction. It is not worth rushing after the crowd. It is not worth looking where the crowd is looking. It is not worth shouting what the crowd shouts. It is not worth mindlessly repeating after the crowd.

"It is worth being yourself. It is worth listening to the heart. It is worth looking with the heart. It is worth trusting yourself. It is worth being a color. The whole color palette. It is worth being a color painter of your own life. It is worth choosing a color instead of a gray crowd and a gray world of fear. It is worth being free. It is worth being different.

"Because the one who trusts himself, the one who befriended himself, the one who is really free, is never lonely. Although apparently, from the level of a gray crowd, he looks different.

"The one who is really free probably goes his own way and knows where he is going. He is not afraid of chaos, wind and storms of this world. A truly free human being walks with trust, confidence and courage. And each step is marked with love. Because love is freedom. Love is Otherness in the gray world of fear."

Fear is a world of obedient, frightened, shouting and fighting among themselves nonentities. A world of stereotypes. A world of inverted values and hypocritical words. A world of war. A world of divisions. A world of control. Matrix.

The world of fear does not like otherness. The world of fear is afraid of otherness. The world of fear tries to trample free, colorful flowers, although it looks at them with curiosity and misses them secretly. In the world of fear, Love is Otherness.

And Love is silence that speaks. Love is a flower. Love is Nature. Love is the earth. Love is water. Love is heaven. Love is air. Love is the Universe. Love is another human being and every other being. Love is You.

Love is a world of beautiful, colorful and free flowers. People are flowers. Only some have forgotten about it. And they have become weeds that suffocate others for their color, freedom and otherness.

Love does not divide. Love does not exclude. Love is not afraid of Otherness. Love accepts and welcomes otherness with open arms. It invites and whispers quietly into your heart,

"I am here. I'm waiting for you. Wake up. Stand up. Come. Remember who you are. Remind yourself that you are a beautiful colorful flower that has only been lost in the gray crowd of fear. I am in You. I am You. You just forgot to water me. You have forgotten to cultivate the flower of Love within you."

NOT EVERYTHING IS LIKE IT SEEMS

Angels and Demons

And it happened once that during my journey called life, I got lost in a dark forest. And this forest was getting denser and denser. Getting darker and darker. I didn't see the path. I couldn't see the light. I couldn't see the door. I wandered in the narrow, cramped, closed corridors of some dark labyrinth of black trees that took on increasingly scary forms. Demons lurked everywhere I looked. And at some point, these corridors became one narrow and dark corridor, going down steeper and steeper. I was falling and collapsing into some rock abyss. A well without water, in which, when falling, I was spinning in circles. And it was getting colder and colder there. Darker and darker. And I was getting weaker and weaker and more and more lost. Increasingly sad.

I didn't have a map. I didn't have a flashlight. I didn't even have a candle or a match. At least that's what I thought at the time. I was alone and very lonely. And the thoughts were terrible. Dark and getting darker. Gloomy. Like the corridor where I was trapped. Thoughts were like worms crawling in the head in all directions and causing chaos of thoughts. The head was heavy with these thoughts. Breasts were squeezed by some iron hoop. It seemed that the heart had been crushed by a pile of stones. Some kind of debris. And I carried more bags of stones on my back and bent under them. I walked slower and slower. Without strength. I felt as if my soul had fallen to pieces. To millions of particles that have scattered throughout the Universe. And I couldn't find them. I couldn't glue them together. I couldn't find myself. Until I finally forgot who I was. My soul fell apart and with it my whole world fell apart.

There were so many demons. And the more I focused on them, the more I wanted to get away from them, the more they cornered me. And there were more and more of them. As if they spontaneously multiplied under the influence of these wormy thoughts. It was enough for me to think of one of them, and he immediately dragged a whole army of more demons with him. And these demons danced their demonic dance around me. And me? I was sitting, or rather lying huddled and terrified. Lonely. Unhappy. Without strength. I pretended to be alive, even though I was dead while I was alive.

And these demons were my past. Little did I know at the time that I had dragged them from the past to my future, which was the present, when in fact it was still the past. Behold, I dwelt among the demons. And I myself became a demon. A demon to myself. I lived in the past and I was the past. But I didn't understand this at the time.

And I was so focused on these demons that I didn't even see that among these dark demons, there were bright figures who reached out to me. As if they wanted to show the way. Help. I ran away from them. I was afraid of the light. I hated my demons, and at the same time I clung to them and didn't want to let go. And instead of light, I chose darkness. Impotence of action. It became more and more difficult to breathe. It became more and more difficult to live. The soul hurt more and more. She cried in me and I cried with her. I wanted to feel nothing. I wanted not to think. I wanted to sleep. I wanted to forget. I wanted to die. And I didn't know I was dead. I was in hell and I hit the bottom of hell. I was in the hell of my own mind.

I wandered through this hell for a long, long time, and even longer. I stopped counting time. Because there is no time in hell. In hell, time seems to be an eternity. It is long, heavy and dark. In hell, time is darkness without end. Because in hell there is only hell. A desert without water and life. No air. No light. Lots of debris, stones and garbage. And a lot of dark demons that for some reason are close. Like friends. You love them and hate them at the same time. You shout in despair, *"Go away! Disappear! Leave me alone!"* And in a moment you run after them and beg, *"Don't leave. Don't leave me. I don't want to be alone."* And you cling to them.

I visited all the dark corners of hell. And since there was no light, I found only some rubble everywhere. I stumbled over stones, fell under those stones, and carried stones. And from under the rubble of stones I pulled out another rubble, and another, and another. Pain. Regret. Rejection. Loneliness. And I believed in all this so much that in the end I myself felt like this unnecessary rubble. I worked hard to move the rubble, gather garbage, and rummage through garbage. And this rubble kept coming and going. Sisyphean work. And even though it was only in my head, I was very, very tired. Thoughts create emotions. Hell is darkness. A cosmic black hole that like a vacuum pulls in all the space garbage to dump it all on your head. Hell is hell. A prison. A garbage can. I became a prisoner of my own mind, even though I didn't know it at the time.

Sometimes at night I would look at the stars. And it was only in these stars that I found temporary solace. And I so immensely missed those stars. Somewhere inside I felt, I knew that this world of earthly hell is not my world. I knew that my real home was somewhere out there. And there is warmth there. Light. Well being. Comfort. And my stellar family is there. My sisters and my brothers. Luminous angels. I wanted to go back there. Tears rolled down my cheeks, and I whispered, "Why did you throw me off here?" Why did you leave me? Why did you leave her alone?"

And one night, when I was looking at the stars, when I was again feeling the pain of my soul being torn to shreds, when tears were flowing from my eyes again, when I felt so very, very lonely and abandoned by everyone, I suddenly turned on another button in the computer of my head. A button under the name: *Phone to a friend*. The button that I just forgot about staring at the demons of darkness. And that friend was myself. And only I could help myself. The button, in fact, was called: *Troubleshooting*. First, however, I had to diagnose this problem. I thought, *"You can't live like that. This is not life. This is hell. I don't want to live like that. I don't want to be in hell. There must be some doors here. There must be a way out. There must be an answer."*

And then I asked myself, *"What are you choosing? Heaven or Hell? You were in Heaven. You know the path. Now you know Hell. What do you choose?"*

"I choose Heaven." I heard my own loud words. Words that came out as if from my inner self. From my soul. And in these words there was great faith and power. There was certainty of what I was saying. I felt it. I was that. I spoke words that were like a spell. They were an intention. They were a choice. They were a decision. They were another button in my head that I hadn't seen before, although I talked about it and thought about it, but while in the dark, I didn't hear or understand my own words that I was uttering myself. I didn't understand my own thoughts. And I didn't understand my own emotions. I couldn't hear my own heart. My soul. My own intuition. Because intuition is the whisper of the soul. The whisper of a luminous angel. I was blind and deaf. I ran away from myself and chased myself. I went around in circles wandering in the depths of the labyrinth of hell.

And when I said those words, magic happened. I felt as if I had opened the door of some invisible cosmic portal. And although this portal was invisible, I saw it. I felt it. I felt it with all of myself. As if communication with the Universe has been restored. With my own soul. After all, the soul is the Universe.

And through this portal answers I was looking for began to flow, not knowing that I was looking for them. *"You are Love. I am Love. I Am."* I heard inside me. These words resounded in me like billions of star bells. And at the same time, I had the impression that these words were sung by the whole Universe. *"I am Love. I Am."* I repeated. And I was relieved. It got so light. I smiled at myself and at the whole Universe. *"I am Love! Yes! I am Love!"* I just forgot about it.

I felt, but I could see that through this invisible, though visible, cosmic door a powerful stream of beautiful golden light is pouring down upon me, which entered me through the top of my head into my heart and filled all of me from within. And it was so good. So good. Serenity. Joy. Happiness. And this enormity of love, which I could not embrace with either my hands or my head. Love wrapped me with its cloak, but at the same time it poured into me and flowed out of me. Everything was One. I was Love and I was in Love. And that was when I woke up from a nightmarish dream. I remembered who I was and why I was here. I was in heaven again, because heaven had come to me. Or maybe it was here all the time, only I didn't see it. Because I didn't want to see.

"I am Love. I am Love. I Am." I repeated happily, and tears ran down my cheeks. Tears of emotion and happiness. I was no longer alone. I had myself. And I had the love of the whole Universe. Because the soul is the Universe. And where there is love, there is life. And I felt that I wanted to live so much, so much, so much. Again, I want to laugh happily. I want to live!

I want to live! I want to live! I want to fly high again! May this moment last!

I wanted to feel again. But this time differently. Knowingly. Wisely. I looked at the trees. They were green again. Beautiful. Alive. Their crowns climbed up to the sky, and smiling leaves danced in the wind.

"Everything is One" I thought. *'But I choose."*

I lay down on the grass. And this grass was green again. Green as grass. I touched it with my hands. I felt roughness and softness at the same time.

"Everything is One" I thought. *'But I choose."*

I looked up at the sky. And that sky was as blue as the sky. And I felt that I am that sky. And in this sky, somewhere far away, a heavy black cloud appeared. It sailed away into the distance. But I no longer focused on that dark cloud. I was looking at the blue.

"Everything is One," I thought. *"But I choose."*

I closed my eyes. The portal reopened again. And here before my eyes, like in a cinema, a movie started screening spontaneously. But as if I was watching it simultaneously from various sides. Multidimensionally. Multi-temporal and multi-spacial. Here I was an observer, a spectator in the audience in the cinema, and at the same time an actor who is in the middle of this film. I was also the director.

I was standing on a hill. In front of me somewhere below, a big field was stretching to the horizon. Like a battlefield. I felt like a general before the battle. I felt the strength of the general. Calmness and concentration. I felt that the fate of this battle in this field depended only on me. And here I saw that an army of soldiers from hell was running towards me, in a tight formation. Small, distorted caricatures of themselves. I saw their horns, their tails, their hooves. They ran towards me, leaving behind a cloud of dust. This sight made me laugh. It reminded me of a computer animation. Of some kind of game. And then a thought came to mind,

"Maybe I am a character from my own computer game. I am a character and a player at the same time? I'm the one who creates this character and I play this character. I create the worlds in which this character moves."

I watched the attackers approaching me and I laughed more and more.

"Do you really think you're going to win with me?" I thought.

But evidently that's what they thought, because they were getting closer fast. And in me there was peace. And such a huge sense of security and strength. I knew that whatever happened or didn't happen, they wouldn't do anything to me. Because they have no power over me. Because I chose heaven. And he who has chosen heaven always has the care of heaven.

And here, for some reason, I thought, *"Michael."* And before I finished thinking, I saw Michael coming down from heaven and holding a sword pointing upwards in his hand. As if he had heard my message. And behind him a whole army of angels of light descended. I looked at him overjoyed, as if I had met my brother. And he looked at me the same way. We looked into each other's eyes as if we had known each other forever. Friends and siblings at the same time. Suddenly, he turned his head for a moment. He looked at the demons swirling in the field and pointed his luminous sword at them. And at that moment, the whole army of darkness turned backwards and began to flee even faster than it had arrived here, leaving behind only clouds of dust that fell on the field. To the ground. And Gaia hugged this dust and turned it into fertile soil.

Michael looked at me again with a smile and love.

"You are my brother." I said, sure of what I was saying.

"Yes." There was serenity in his voice and a kind of joy due to the fact that I met him.

"Will you sometimes lend me your sword?" I asked.

"It's yours." He replied by stretching out his hand towards me, in which he held a luminous sword. *"Use it wisely."*

And then I understood how powerful thought is. Because thought creates. It is enough to change the thought, and the whole reality around me changes. My world is changing, and I am changing. Because a change in thought changes perception. The character I play is changing. And my goal as a player playing this game with this particular character and this particular character, which after all I am myself, is to reach the highest level in this game. And each subsequent higher level activates new skills. Thought is like a keyboard in the computer of the head, but I decide which key to press. I understood what I knew before, but I didn't seem to understand. I realized that I was the one creating. I'm the one holding the joystick in my hand. I have the power to create. I create my darkness and my light. My angels and demons. And all this is One, but I am choosing. I realized that what I was thinking, what I was talking about, what I was focusing on, I am attracting and experiencing. Because everything is energy. Similar attracts similar.

And I realized that my whole life is really going on in my head. And what I see is the illusion of a computer game. I realized that everything I had experienced and was experiencing was an illusion. A hologram. It is an energetic reflection of my beliefs and convictions. I realized that this character in the battlefield game is really fighting herself. And this struggle takes place within herself. Within me. I am my best friend and my worst enemy at the same time. I am an angel and a demon. And it is I who choose.

I also understood that the doors of the portal connecting me to the Universe have always been where they are. Only I didn't want to see them. Because I didn't really want to open them. I closed myself off to the whisper of my own soul. I focused on darkness, and I saw only darkness. And I didn't want to see anything else. I became a prisoner of my own darkness. My dark thoughts. My past, which I clung to so tightly. I forgot about my luminous sword of Strength, which I always had. I gave up my sword and laid myself on the sacrificial table. I became a prisoner of my own mind. I blamed others for this darkness, but I did it to myself. Me alone. Because I stopped trusting myself. I stopped believing myself. My heart. My intuition. My soul. I stopped loving myself. I stopped trusting In Love. Love flowing from the Source of Love. Love that loves unconditionally. Love, which is freedom. Love, which is Light. Love, which is my Strength. My Michael's sword, but after all mine.

I was the one who created all these dark demons. I let them into my house and fed them with my dark, wormy thoughts. And while feeding the demons, I starved myself. I gave my power to the demons. I took love away from myself and closed myself off to love. I focused on demons. And what you focus on grows. I pushed myself into hell. I became a prisoner of hell. And being in the prison of darkness, I forgot who I was. I forgot where I came from and where I was going. I forgot that I am the Light. I forgot about my sword, about my strength. I forgot that the only way out of hell is the way up. And that's what I recalled.

The moment I chose Heaven was the moment of awakening from a deep, nightmarish dream. The moment when I found the stairs to Heaven. My decision to move out of Hell and live in Heaven marked the beginning of a new stage in my journey called life. The beginning of a new path that began at the very bottom of hell. The beginning of hard work on yourself. And this beginning was difficult. Because I was still in hell full of stones and rubble that I was tripping over. And there were still demons there. And these demons did not disappear immediately. They existed and did not let go so easily. But now I looked at them differently and saw them differently. And I had the impression that they were asking for something. And the more they asked, the more they clung to me. And I, a million times a day, repeated to myself the phrase I once heard,

"When you go through hell, do not stop. Go. Someday it will end."

And I was determined to get through this hell as soon as possible. I didn't want to be there for a nanosecond longer than necessary.

And now when I woke up and got my sword back, it turned out that it's not so dark in this hell. As if someone had turned on a light in it. Powerful light. And I understood that that light is me. And in that light, I saw that hell has colors and is not so terrible at all. Well! As soon as I illuminated the dark corners, it turned out a lot of beautiful things were hidden there that I had simply not seen before. I understood that by bringing darkness to the light, I was discovering what had been hidden so far. I am getting to know the Universe. I am getting to know the mystery of which I am a part.

I also found a map. I found my inner GPS, which is my heart. My intuition. My inner voice, which I had not listened to before. An angel who points the way and whispers quietly,

"Your only task in this life is to be happy."

But when you happen to turn off navigation, it's easy to get lost in the dark forest. The head screams loudly as if it wants to be louder than everything and louder than itself. But for some reason, it is the heart that always knows what is best for you.

When I recalled who I was and knew where I was going, while walking through this hell I was no longer huddled. I walked with my head held high. Still barefoot, but in spurs. I put on my shoes later. But I was the one who chose those shoes and consciously chose the path I was on. I walked boldly and attentively. I walked with the curiosity of a child who gets to know the world. And learning to walk anew in this new world, which opened up to consecutive rooms, each of which was more beautiful than the previous one, I sometimes stopped, sometimes stumbled over old rubble and sometimes fell. Sometimes the darkness squeezed by the throat and the demons pulled backwards. But I already knew how it worked, even though I was still learning myself. And I understood more and more what free will was.

I learned to forgive and I forgave. And each forgiveness was like throwing off a few tons of ballast. It was another step up on my journey to heaven. By forgiving and letting go of the past, I freed myself from the pain. And each forgiveness turned the angel of darkness into a beautiful angel of light who smiled at me with joy, love and gratitude. Because that's what the angels of darkness asked me to do. They asked for forgiveness. Forgiving, I freed them from the costume of a dark robe that turned white. The angels could return to heaven. They did the job that I asked them to do. By releasing my demons, I was releasing myself. Forgiveness is the key to delivering from hell.

On this journey through hell, I understood the power of gratitude. I understood that gratitude is the key to abundance.

My pass to Paradise. I understood that pain is when there are expectations. I exchanged expectations for gratitude. And with gratitude, I release what I no longer need and make room for the new one that comes and manifests in Abundance. And with gratitude I accept this New. Gratitude is the key to the gates of paradise.

And once, looking up at the starry sky, I listened to the music of the stars. And suddenly I heard myself saying in a surprised voice to myself,

"How light my head is."

And then I realized that thoughts weigh. And a lot. I realized that the lighter the thoughts, the lighter and more enjoyable the journey.

I looked gratefully at the stars. And these stars blinked at me, talked to me, sang for me, and danced their stellar dance for me. And I felt harmony. Balance. Unity. I felt that my body, my soul and my head were one. The Holy Trinity. And I felt myself flowing and dancing to the rhythm of this stellar music. I spin in the most beautiful tone. Vibration of the energy of Love. And these stars were with me and in me and around me. They were everywhere. And I was one of them. I was a star drop in the evaluation of the energy of the Universe, and I was the whole ocean. I was everything and nothing at the same time.

I am a star drop in the evaluation of the energy of the Universe and I am the whole ocean. I am everything and nothing at the same time.

Now, when I sit on the shore of the ocean and look at the horizon, there is only this moment of Now. There is no yesterday, no tomorrow. It is only Now. The past has remained in the past. The future is a mystery. And my life goes on now. At this point, Now. I look at a tree and I am that tree. I look at a bird and I'm that bird. I look at the water and I am that water. I touch the earth and I am the earth. I meet another human being and I am that human being. Because the other human being is just a different version of me. And sometimes, this human being is lost in his journey, just as I was. And then I tell him my story.

"... And it happened once that during my journey called life, I got lost in a dark forest. I got lost and went to hell. I fell into the darkness where I met many demons. And in this hell, it was cold. Because there was no love there. There was no light. I died. And when I died, I chose life. I chose freedom. I chose myself. I chose love. And when I did, I was resurrected. I found the stairs to heaven. I found myself. I understood that the demons were demons because, like me, they were lost in the darkness. And like me, they desired light. They desired warmth. They desired love."

Angels and Demons. An illusion in itself. Like two but one. Thanks to demons, I found myself, got to know myself and returned to myself. Thanks to demons, I remembered who I was. I remembered my wings, which I had hidden in my backpack. And when I spread them out, it turned out that they are beautiful, big and strong. More beautiful, bigger and stronger than I could have imagined. And thanks to these wings, I was able to fly to the stars. To heaven. And this is heaven, as if it came down to me. Here, to the ground. Thanks to demons, I understood what absolute love is. Demons turned out to be my best teachers. Because sometimes something has to hurt for us to notice it. And when I gratefully hugged them, black angels turned into angels of light. Thanks to demons I came to know angels and dwelt in heaven among angels. Thanks to demons I became an angel myself. Heaven and hell are a state of mind. Perception creates our reality.

The journey through hell turned out to be the most interesting journey of my life. The most difficult, but also the most sublime and instructive. After all, we learn by experiencing. Now I'm talking about the blessing of depression, although not everyone understands it. But those who have gone through a similar path and understood their lessons look at it similarly and speak similarly. They smile and shine like the most beautiful stars. They spread around them this wonderful glow of the energy of love, which magnetizes with its beauty. They don't chase love. They do not run away from love. They are love. Because love is the path, the truth and the life. People call them angels.

I fell under the heavy cross many times. And although I was seemingly alone, I was never alone. I just didn't always want to see a helping hand extended towards me. Sometimes it was a word, sometimes a smile, sometimes a gesture, and sometimes it was just someone's faith in me. Presence without words. But it was precisely this silence that gave solace.

The angels smiled at me and whispered quietly,

"Choose love. Trust yourself. Trust your heart. Your only task in this life is to be happy."

The angels showed the way, but they respected my choices. My free will. The demons did demonic things. But in a way, they also respected my choices. After all, I chose this darkness and wormy thoughts myself. They only gave me what I chose. And they also showed me the way. Because these demons seem to be saying,

"What else do we need to do to finally make you remember who you are? How much more hell do we have to throw on your head so that you can get out of hell. To trust yourself. To make you love yourself. To draw your sword of Strength. To choose love. Because only with love can you disenchant yourself and disenchant us. Only love will lead you out of hell."

Thanks to this journey through hell, I returned to the stars. Once I got lost in a dark forest. But sometimes you have to get lost to find yourself. Thanks to the demons, I understood that not everything is like it seems to us.

arek-art.de

Acknowledgment

I would like to especially thank my translator **Elizabeth Kanski** for her support and excellent translation that reflects my original language style and the atmosphere of my stories.

Many thanks, **Marek Szczęsny** for the beautiful painting of the book cover, which he specially painted, and for sharing his other pictures, which make the graphic design of this book more attractive.
https://www.facebook.com/mars0510

Also, I want to say thank **Kay Umland** for her involvement in the beautiful cover design.
https://www.deviantart.com/theartofkay

Thank you, friends.

And thank **You, Dear Reader.** Thank you for trusting when you bought this book and thank you for reading this book. Thank you for accepting the invitation to my world, which is also your world. And we create this world together. I believe that these stories showed you, that it is no need to rush with judgment. Usually, NOT EVERYTHING IS LIKE IT SEEMS.

Katarzyna Nowocin-Kowalczyk, author

www.ingramcontent.com/pod-product-compliance
Lightning Source LLC
Chambersburg PA
CBHW060453300726
48975CB00008B/2497